DEVIL IN THE DARK WOODS

MARK GILLESPIE

JOIN THE READER LIST

If you enjoy what you read here and want to be notified whenever there's a new book out, join the reader list. Just click the link below. It'll only take a minute.

www.markgillespieauthor.com

(The sign up box is on the Home Page)

You can also follow Mark on Bookbub.

1

———

Mike's reflexes were on point tonight. And thank God for that, he thought, as for the third time straight, a Japanese-themed designer coffee cup flew through the air at a hundred miles per hour. Aimed at his head.

The cup missed Mike's left temple by inches. He winced as it slammed into the tiled wall at his back, then landed on the kitchen floor minus a handle.

Anita's aim was improving with each throw. She was standing on the other side of the kitchen, already armed with the next weapon. This time it was a teacup. Salviati Murano. Her arm was semi-cocked like a pitcher intent on making the throw of her life – the speed of light, and nothing else would do. She's moving onto the good stuff, Mike thought. Jesus, it had been almost an hour since they'd left the restaurant and Anita's volcanic temper was still at full boil. He felt like Pompeii to her Vesuvius. She was glaring at Mike as she had been almost non-stop for the past hour, her taut frame squeezed into a high-necked, white dress that showed off her exquisitely toned arms. Her blue elfin eyes burned. Her cheeks sizzled red as Mike imagined spirals of steam emanating from her long blonde hair.

Mike glanced down at the ceramic graveyard gathering at his feet. "Are you done yet? Can we start behaving like adults now?"

Anita's laugh was full of scorn. "No. As a matter of fact, *Mike*, I'm not done yet."

"What the hell is wrong with you?" Mike asked, still trying to keep his voice at a reasonable level. *Keep calm and carry on.* "Are you seriously doing this right now?"

The Murano cup trembled in Anita's grip. "Stop trying to turn this back on me," she yelled. "I saw the way you looked at her tonight. I saw the lust spilling out of your eyes you horny motherfucker. Why do you keep trying to skip over that one crucial detail, huh?"

Mike sighed. "Crucial detail? What crucial detail?"

"Lust. You were lusting over that woman tonight and doing it right in front of me. Right in front of me for God's sake."

"You're still talking about the waitress?" Mike said. "You're running with that one all the way to the end, huh?" He slapped a hand over his mouth, then took it away. "Nothing happened Anita. Okay? Nothing happened. You're mad because I was courteous to the waitress in the restaurant? Holy shit. This is crazy."

"What's the matter stud?" Anita said, pacing the room like a wildcat locked in a cage. "You don't like white women anymore? Got a hankering for one of your own?"

Mike spat out an involuntary gust of laughter. It was a mistake and he barely dodged the flying Murano. This one hit the wall with a loud nasty crack before shattering into half a dozen pieces, most of which ended up in the sink.

"That's it," Anita said. "Isn't it? Just tell me. You're trying to get it on with one of your own, aren't you?"

Mike scratched his head. "One of my own? Oh right, I get it. The waitress was black and I'm black and that automatically means we're tribal fuck-buddies, right? Great job Anita, are you fucking kidding me right now? You wanna know what I was doing tonight? I saw a woman working her ass off in that restaurant, pushing through a tough shift and having to deal with entitled assholes like us because their starters weren't on the table ten seconds after they ordered them. Because their desserts weren't served at precisely five degrees. Did you hear some of those people in there, the way they talked to her? I saw that and I made a point of being nice to that woman. Hang me, why don't you?"

"Nice to her?" Anita said, her pacing coming to a sudden stop. "You might as well have put a ring on her finger Mike. I was starting to feel like a fifth wheel in there, you know what I mean? Like I was getting in the way."

"Bullshit," Mike snapped. "I looked her in the eye. I spoke to her like a human being – you were there for God's sake. I let her know that I appreciated what she was doing and so yeah, I smiled at her. Big fucking deal. I gave her a generous tip in hand because she damn well earned it and I didn't want it ending up in the manager's pocket. That's what I did – I showed her some respect and for that reason alone you start laying into me like I ripped her clothes off in front of you. And you're still going strong over an hour later. Oh man, you're messed up Anita. Tell me something, are your sisters as hotheaded as you are? Do Lindy and Roz act like they belong in a padded cell every time their partners tip the Uber driver?"

Anita pulled out a chair from the dining table. The legs

shrieked as they scraped off the porcelain floor. She sat down in a hurry, elbows on the table, staring at the walls. Chest heaving.

"Fucking men. Be straight with me Mike. If it wasn't 'cos she's black, was it the uniform? Is that what turned you on? You like that working-class girl thing now you're hot shit?"

Mike groaned. "You're insane."

"And you're a prick," Anita said. There was so much fire in her eyes that Mike was starting to sweat. He felt her stare pushing him back against the countertop.

"How can you be this insecure?" he asked. "I don't understand it. You're one third of Flaming Candy, the biggest pop band in the world. You cut records with your sisters and some of the finest producers out there and you do it all in the best recording studios in the world. You tour everywhere. You got all this going for you at the age of twenty-four, all the money you'll ever need and a house to die for in upstate New York. And you're insecure because I smiled at another woman? A woman who's probably working two jobs, maybe more, maybe she's got kids to feed and maybe, just maybe she needed to know tonight that she wasn't just a *thing* moving plates and glasses back and forth at Club Asshole. We're lucky Anita – do you know how lucky we are to do what we do? But not everyone else is as lucky. You gotta remember that or you'll lose touch with reality."

The kitchen filled with silence.

"You're a big deal," Anita said, stabbing a fork gently into the wooden table. Mike felt every one of those hits like the prongs were going into his neck. "Movie director, Oscar winner, chicks dig that kind of thing. And you know it."

"Dig?" Mike said, screwing up his face. "What the hell? Are you auditioning for a blaxploitation movie now?"

"Fuck off. I can say whatever I want. You think that waitress didn't know who she was waiting on tonight?"

Mike shrugged. He kicked away a piece of stray ceramic at his feet so that it landed beside the rest of the pile.

"Yeah, I'm sure she recognized me. I'm sure she was also planning to kidnap me right after coffee and mints and that she had a van with blacked out windows and a full tank of gas running in the parking lot. I'm sure she had it all. Shit, if she was going to recognize anyone Anita, it would have been you. Your face is a lot more familiar than mine."

"What about those dumb fucking superhero movies you started making?" Anita said. "Everyone knows them."

She might as well have stabbed the fork into Mike's heart.

"They know the actors," he said in a quiet voice. "Not so much the director."

"They are kinda dumb though. Aren't they Mike?"

"Thanks a lot Anita," he said. "Please spare me the *Mike-Harvey-sold-his-soul* monologue, thank you very much. I get enough of that everywhere else and for the record, there's absolutely nothing wrong with a little popcorn entertainment. If a movie, any type of movie, makes someone happy then it's a good thing."

Anita stood up, letting the fork fall onto the table. She folded her arms tight across her chest. "So are you going to apologize?"

Mike stared at her, waiting for the punchline. When it didn't come, he made a brief brushing aside motion with his hand.

"Fuck this," he said. "There's no trust here anymore. Don't you see it? Every time we talk I feel like I'm having a conversation with a stick of dynamite."

Mike turned towards the kitchen door, although he was

still looking at Anita. "What do you think? Should we call it a day on this? On...us?"

Anita shook her head. Her voice was the calmest it had been all night. "Don't even think about it Mike."

"Or what? I'm already thinking about it."

He walked over to the countertop and pulled a kitchen knife out of the wooden stand. He offered it, handle first, to Anita.

"When there are no more cups and plates to throw," he said. "Is this what comes next? One, two, maybe three months from now?"

Anita didn't say anything. Her head continued to sway from side to side in that slow, mechanical rhythm.

Mike slid the knife back into the stand. "I'm done," he said with a final sigh. "I don't need this domestic bullshit in my life. Been there, done that and bought the t-shirt."

He smiled sadly.

"It's over."

He walked towards the kitchen door. Despite the heavy feeling in his heart, Mike felt an urgency to get out of the house and fast. He slipped through the open doorway, into the hallway. Why did he have to show her the knife for God's sake? Dumb move, especially now that he'd exposed his back to her. Anita still had time to run to the stand, grab the biggest mother in the rack, chase after Mike and plunge that thing deep into him, all the way to the bone, before he could reach the front door.

Crazy, Mike thought. You're thinking crazy thoughts. She's not a monster. She's a pop star. And yet the voice in his head was crystal clear.

GET OUT.

NOW.

Mike walked and kept walking. One step at a time, with all the fluidity of a mannequin trying to escape the store. Out of the kitchen, down the long – very long – hallway. There was the door. Keep going, keep going. He didn't hear footsteps behind him, thank God. His hand was trembling as it grappled with the door handle and thank you again God, Mike thought, because the door wasn't locked.

He stepped outside, closing the door behind him. He was calm, surprisingly so. The cool, night air tasted good and why not?

Still, it wasn't over. Not until he was out of there for real, far from Anita's property. Mike hurried across the driveway to where he'd parked the Genius Car.

He stopped beside the car, his fingers gripping the handle. The Genius had been a gift from Anita, back when they'd celebrated one month of going out together. That felt like a long time ago when she'd splashed out big time (although it would barely have made a dent in her bank account) and bought Mike the latest thing in automobile luxury. There were only about twelve hundred Genius Cars in existence and damn, Mike loved it. The gadgets were off the charts, the handling was super smooth, and three months down the line everything was tuned to perfection. The car fit Mike like a glove. But if he took it now, after breaking up with her like he'd just done, it meant there was still a connection. That didn't work. If he was serious about breaking things off, he'd leave the car and figure out some other way to get back to the city.

"Damn it," he said, his fingers still on the metal handle.

He stood there, looking back and forth between the house and the car.

"What do I do?"

Leaving the car would be the right thing to do. Wouldn't it? That would be the honorable thing to do – to walk away, sever all ties and it would send the right message; it would let Anita know that he was serious about calling it quits. But he liked the car. *Loved* the car. It was slick as hell in more ways than one and that was understating the matter. Moving onto more practical and immediate concerns, it was a forty-minute drive back to New York City from the outskirts of Scarsdale. How else was he supposed to get home? Hitch? He sure as hell wasn't in the mood to make small talk with a cab driver or an Uber driver. Not tonight.

Say, ain't you the guy who killed off Black Jaguar?

Mike's heart skipped a beat as the front door of the house opened and then slammed shut behind him. Sounded like a T. rex thundering over the gravel driveway. Coming in fast.

"Oh shit."

He swiveled his body so that he was facing Anita's six-million-dollar luxury home, silhouetted and so monstrously big that it devoured the landscape.

She hurried towards him, arms stiff and robotic. Mike's blood cooled and in the absence of any light other than the meek spotlights lining the driveway, he couldn't tell for sure if there was anything in her hand. Not yet.

"You don't just walk out on someone like that," Anita said. "We're not done yet."

Mike pulled the keys out of his back pocket, hit the unlock button and pulled the car door open. It was time to go and to hell with it – he was taking the car.

"We *are* done."

He dropped into the passenger seat, desperate to get moving. The freedom of the road was calling Mike Harvey home and he was ready to answer the call. Even if Anita had no intention of sticking a sharp blade in his back, she could always slash the tires in a bid to keep him there. She'd paid for the car after all.

Mike lowered the driver's side window. "Anita, just go back in the house. Okay? We both need to chill out and give each other some space."

Anita's blue eyes were unusually bright in the dark. Glowing. And as she got closer to the Genius Car, Mike saw that there *was* something in her hand. But it wasn't the knife. It was the samurai sword that she kept on display on the living room wall. It wasn't just an ornament either. Mike knew for a fact that Anita paid good money for a local sword nutcase to come to the house and sharpen that mother on a regular basis. Home security, that's what she called it.

"You wanna get ghetto?" Anita said, the gleaming katana tip pointing at Mike's face. "I can do that. You think I'm some sort of spoiled little rich girl who's afraid to get her hands dirty, don't you? Well we can get fucking crazy if that's what you want Mikey babe. I'm ready to spill some blood. Get out of the car now!"

Mike stared at her as if she'd sprouted a third leg. "C'mon Anita, get a grip." He pointed down the driveway towards the exit. "There's probably a bunch of Flaming Candy groupies hanging around the gate filming this on their phones. You want this all over YouTube in the morning? What will your mother say when you drag your squeaky clean image through the mud?"

"Get out the car Mike."

Mike shook his head and started the engine. "Take a deep breath," he said over the soft, welcoming hum of the Genius. "Take several in fact. And start acting like a fucking grown up while you're at it, okay Anita? Ghetto? Ghetto for Christ's sake? You don't even know how to be racist, do you?"

"GET OUT THE FUCKING CAR!"

Anita was pretty much breathing fire by now. She charged forward and Mike hit the gas. The Genius tore down the driveway, panicked tires spitting a hail of stones and debris in their wake. Sounded like he'd just robbed the place. Mike hoped Anita wouldn't chase after the car because he still had to stop at the front gate and punch in the code before he could get back on the main road. Anita's security staff changed the code every week but fortunately for Mike, he remembered the current numbers from picking her up earlier that night.

"Eight, nine, two, one, one, seven," he said. "Eight, nine, two, one, one, seven."

It was quiet as Mike pulled up at the wrought iron gate. Thank God, there were no Flaming Candy Instagram or Tik-Tok all-stars hanging around, waiting for a glimpse of their idol. Maybe an autograph. Maybe a millisecond of eye contact. Must have been their night off or something.

Mike opened the door, hurried out and punched in the six-figure code. His heart pounded in the interval between typing in the numbers and waiting for the flashing green light that meant all good to go. The gate creaked opened and he ran back towards the car.

He stopped before climbing into the driver's seat, taking a last look towards the house.

His girlfriend, *ex-girlfriend*, was a silhouette in the drive-way. The massive house made for an eerie backdrop and although it was a modern building dating back only eight years, it had all the vibes of a haunted castle.

Anita called out, but Mike didn't hear what she said. He didn't want to hear it either.

They were done. Two people at the crossroads of their

life, moving in opposite directions. It had been fun, no doubt about that, but it was over.

Mike got back in the car and drove through the exit. As he watched the gate close over in the rearview mirror, he breathed a sigh of relief.

Thank Christ that's over, he thought.

2

———

It felt good to Mike, putting distance between himself and the house. He nodded at the anxious face in the rearview, reassuring his reflection that it was okay. He'd done the right thing.

"All because I was nice to someone," he said. "Can you believe that?"

Man, she'd flown off the handle. And sure, Mike had heard rumors about Anita long before they hooked up and became an item. Not from journalists or the gossipmongers on social media, but from the people who knew her – from those who'd been in the Flaming Candy inner circle for a long time. They weren't shy in spilling the beans either, at least not in private and certainly not after a few drinks. Assistants mostly, people at the beck and call of Anita, Lindy and Roz Gordon, not to mention their manager-mom, Martha. People who'd had more than their fair share of the pampered pop star shit and were ready to unload. Mike had first come into contact with Flaming Candy and their staff on the LA party scene, usually at some awards show or a well-publicized charity thing. Anita was all over him, lavishing him with praise about his movies. During those early days, some of the insiders had pulled Mike aside and in their best I'm-trying-to-do-you-a-favor voice, told him that Flaming Candy's squeaky-clean image was a flaming load of bull crap. The girls were walking nightmares and so was their mother. Beware, they said. Proceed with caution.

But Mike didn't listen to any of the warnings. In fact, he liked that contrast of the clean image on top and danger lurking underneath the surface. And what red-blooded guy didn't like the story of the good girl turned bad? Best of all, Anita was nothing like Tracey, his ex-wife. The slow death of that marriage, childhood sweethearts falling out of love and taking far too long to admit it to themselves let alone each other, was something Mike longed to put behind him. Anita was a breath of fresh air and she came into Mike's life at the right time. She was thirteen years younger than he was – twenty-four, with the energy of a small child on a sugar rush. After those early meetings in LA and New York, it had been a whirlwind romance and Mike had to admit, it was fun being part of a celebrity couple, at least at the start anyway. He was at the height of his profession and so was Anita. The cameras loved them and everything was too damn easy.

As the relationship progressed, Mike saw Anita's dark side emerging in small doses. The rumors it turned out, weren't just rumors. Her cocaine habit would put most old school rock stars to shame. She made Tony Montana look like a monk. But even though it had scared Mike a little, it had excited him too. She didn't try to hide it from him either, even though he had no desire to snort the Bolivian marching powder himself. Mike Harvey was old school. He liked liquor and yeah, he liked calling it liquor too. Anita thought that was cute.

It was never meant to last. They were two very different people whose paths had crossed for a little while. They'd had fun and that was enough.

Mike had to get out of Scarsdale. Put it all behind him and drive back to New York City, bachelor life, no commitments and sure as hell no long-term relationships with anything besides his work. First step, get the Genius onto the Bronx River Parkway and on the road back to Tribeca, Manhattan. Back to his peaceful apartment. A glass of Scotch, a double of course, before calling it a day. And what a day.

The panel beeped, alerting Mike to an incoming video call. He glanced at the display, already knowing whose face he'd see and sure enough there was Anita's photo flashing up on the screen. That white-toothed heavenly smile, so innocent.

Why couldn't she just let him go? She was young, beautiful and she could have anyone she wanted. But that's not how it worked, right?

He looked at the screen again, hesitating. Hoping that the call would stop by itself and take the decision out of his hands.

It kept ringing.

Mike groaned and pushed the green button. He kept his camera switched off, opting for audio only. His eyes were locked on the road, searching for the signs to the parkway. It was dark out tonight, so it seemed. Not quite regular dark.

"Hey Anita," he said without enthusiasm.

"Mike," she said, swallowing loud and hard. Sounded like she'd been crying just before he picked up. "Put the camera on, will you? I can't see you."

"No. That's not a good idea."

"Why not?"

A pause.

"Well," Mike said, rummaging for the right words. "I'm driving for starters and it's real dark out here."

"It's a Genius Car," Anita said. There was a hint of the old fire in her voice again. "Turn on the self-drive and talk to me properly. Please Mike, this is serious shit and I'm really scared right now. And I'm all alone."

"Not a good idea," Mike repeated.

"Please."

"No. Listen to me Anita – we were both pretty worked up back there at the house. But this, uhh, this outcome, it's for the best. It really is."

Boy, he was bad at this. At least with Tracey they'd both wanted out of the marriage and in the end, neither one of them cared enough to have an argument about it. There was only relief at the inevitable parting when it came.

"I want to apologize for being such a bitch," Anita said. "Some of the things I said earlier were horrible."

"I appreciate that," Mike said, visualizing the samurai sword in her hand. "But let's weigh things up with calmer heads, shall we? It's been a great four months and I really mean that. Still, it's time to call it quits. Don't you think this thing has run its natural course?"

He heard Anita exhale on the other end of the line. Mike could almost feel her warm breath escaping through the speakers, spraying all over his skin. He looked at the clock. Almost midnight. Time to go home.

"I was out of line," Anita said. "And I can totally see where you're coming from. I can. How you were just being nice to that waitress tonight. Like, it makes sense when you stop and think about it. I don't know what's wrong with me babe. Sometimes the anger gets out before I even know it's there."

Mike felt a stab of guilt. Now she was starting to sound like a grown-up.

"Yeah," he said. "I hear you Anita, but that temper of yours – it's something you have to face up to or someday it'll consume you and everything in your path. And hey, there's no shame in asking for help, right? No shame at all. You got a few months before the European tour starts. Maybe that's something you could throw yourself into for a while in between rehearsals."

"Yeah," Anita said. "I guess. And say I went through with something like that, would you reconsider...?"

Mike jumped in quick. "I didn't mean it like that. I'm sorry."

There was a long pause. Mike looked at the dash and saw her picture still grinning at him. She hadn't hung up.

"Anita?" he asked.

"Hey Mike," she said. "Do you remember what we did that night? Back at the beginning when I said we were joined forever?"

Mike grimaced in the rearview, both the one in the car and the one in his head. It gave him the chills just thinking about that night, two or three weeks into the relationship when things, although growing more serious, had still been new and exciting. It happened in a hotel room in LA. At Anita's insistence, they'd drank a drop of each other's blood. It was creepy and it had freaked him out a little, but Mike went along with it because he was still trying to prove to the young, vibrant Anita that he wasn't a square whose best days were behind him. She'd cut them both on the thumb, the blood dripping into a gothic-looking vial that she just happened to have in her suitcase. He remembered watching her doing it, methodical, not a hint of discomfort in her eyes and thinking that she'd done it before. And he recalled the words that she'd spoken after the drinking.

"Now we are unbroken. Now we are one."

That night had never come up again. Mike had always been waiting for it to rear its ugly head in conversation but it never had. Until now.

"We were just fooling around," Mike said.

"I wasn't," Anita said. "We can't be broken Mike. We *can't* be."

"Listen I know you don't want to hear this," Mike said, searching for those elusive road signs to the parkway. "But we *are* broken. It's been on the cards for a while, you know? There's no point in dragging it out any longer. It's a waste of time for both of us."

She was crying now.

"On the cards for a while? That's news to me."

Mike was beginning to feel bad for leaving her alone in the house. Maybe he should have stuck around her place longer, talked it through face to face and let her cry it out on his shoulder. That was probably the decent thing to do, but then again, she'd thrown everything in the kitchen in his face before chasing after him with a samurai sword and what looked like a genuine desire to spill blood. If he'd stuck around there's every chance that Anita would've turned him into a sushi filling for sure. No, he'd done the right thing getting out of there. When Anita's temper was on full throttle there was no happy ending. A shame too. When she was happy, Anita was a joyful presence to be around. She was generous to a fault too and her sense of humor, although dark and cutting, was undeniably hilarious.

"I can't lose you Mike," she said, sniffing loudly. "Just the thought of someone else touching you makes me feel physically sick. I don't think I can cope with it. Look, all that ghetto stuff I was running my mouth off with in the driveway – it was just the rage talking. It was crazy. I'm a fucking psycho, I know that. You know I didn't mean any of it. I'm not a real racist or whatever, you know that right?"

"Uh, yeah."

Thank God she couldn't see his face. The ghetto. Jesus H. Christ. Mike Harvey had never set foot in a real ghetto in his life. He'd grown up in Tribeca, Manhattan, the son of a federal judge and an anthropologist/author. He went to Columbia, joined the rat race for five minutes before deciding to turn his back on the rats and pursue his passion of filmmaking instead of a law degree. What did he know about the ghetto?

Eddie. Don't that make you think of Eddie?

There was always the long shadow cast by Mike's elder brother Eddie, who'd enjoyed all the same advantages that Mike had growing up. Eddie had been a smart kid, but all that intelligence and good upbringing wasn't enough to save him in the end. The cop that pulled Eddie over didn't see any of the advantages or the good manners that the Harveys had instilled in their eldest boy. He saw a ghetto rat in upper-middle class clothing because that's what he wanted to see. Or that's what he'd been programmed to see even though he probably told everyone, like Anita had just told Mike, that he wasn't a racist. Mike had seen those exact words printed in a newspaper clipping that his dad had kept and buried in a set of drawers in the spare bedroom. It had always bothered Mike what those journalist a-holes printed about Eddie in order to make it seem like the shooting was Eddie's fault and not the fault of thirty-three-year-old Cecil Proudfoot, the Jersey cop who'd fucked up at the side of the road. Mike had never told Anita about the clippings or any of the one-sided press reports that he'd discovered in the years following Eddie's death as he'd grown older and more curious about the case. She'd just pulled the 'ghetto' word out of a hat, not knowing that it always took Mike back to Eddie and the bullshit circus that surrounded his death. Correction, his murder.

"Look," Mike said, trying to keep his focus on the conversation at hand. *Where the hell were all the road signs out here?* "We had a great four months. We had a lot of fun, right? But now it's time to move on – you got your music, your touring, recording, your TV appearances and all the rest of it to keep you going. I got my movies and writing. We're busy people Anita and we're both in crazy industries that don't let us stay at home much. We would've drifted apart sooner or later. You gotta trust me on that."

There was a long, uncomfortable silence but Anita's picture remained on the dash. Mike heard the clinking of glass through the speakers. The sloshing noise of liquid being poured clumsily into a glass. He couldn't bring himself to hang up on her, not yet. But still, he had to concentrate on the road. He couldn't find the damn parkway even though he was taking the same route from Anita's house back to the city that he always took. But it was so dark tonight. The streetlights were losing the fight and by now, Mike was pretty sure that he was lapping the outskirts of Scarsdale.

Anita's voice pulled him back to the call.

"Mike?"

"Yeah?"

"If you break up with me, I'll tell my dad."

Mike raised his eyebrows. "Woah. You'll tell your dad?"

Anita had rarely spoken about her father before, in private or in public. All he knew was that the old man had been a fleeting presence in her mother's life about twenty-five years ago and that he'd taken a walk before the triplets were born. Probably the old line about going out for a pack of cigarettes and then never coming back. The only thing Mike remembered Anita saying about her dad was that he lived somewhere down south.

"Did you really just say that?" Mike asked, his voice up an octave with the shock.

"I mean it Mike. And trust me when I say you don't want my dad involved."

"Oh, you mean it?" Mike said. Holy shit, the poor girl needed serious help if she was resorting to this line of attack. *Daddy's going to kick your ass!* Samurai swords and phantom fathers. Mike was already debating whether to call her Martha Gordon and tell her that Anita needed psychiatric treatment or she'd be dead by thirty. Not surprising when you think about it. The triplets had been pushed into the spotlight from an early age and never had a say in their own destiny. Such was the price of chasing someone else's dream of fame and riches. In this case, their mother's dream.

"I'm supposed to be scared?" Mike asked. "Scared of a guy you don't even know?"

Anita laughed. That made Mike nervous.

"I never said I didn't know my dad. What I said was that I didn't have much contact with him. That's not the same thing."

"Whatever," Mike said. "Do what you have to do. I'm hanging up the phone Anita. Over and..."

"I'd be very careful if I were you," Anita said, cutting him off in a stern tone. She sounded older than her years. "I'd be very careful about your next move Mike. About what you say and do."

Mike strained his eyes and the road responded by darkening further. He pulled the Genius through a tight curve and noticed there wasn't a lot of light ahead, except for the two headlights grappling with night. Looked to Mike like the entire state of New York was teetering on the brink of a blackout.

"I get it," he said. "Daddy's going to come to my house and beat me up. Jesus, Anita – you've regressed to fourteen years old because we've broken up. Are we still in junior high or what?"

Anita's voice sounded closer. "Come back to the house. Turn the car around and we'll talk about this."

"Listen," Mike said, unable to contain the irritation in his voice. That irritation was fueled both by Anita's immaturity and the lack of directions on the road. He was going to have to use the GPS on his phone, which seemed an odd thing to do for a journey he supposedly knew like the back of his hand. And yet, he was lost.

"It's over. This is NOT up for discussion anymore. I'm ending this call, right here, right now. Please Anita, take a few days and let it sink in. I promise, you won't give a damn about me by the end of the week. You'll think I'm an asshole and that's fine. Okay? I'm hanging up now."

"Not okay. Not FUCKING okay!"

"Listen," Mike said, his index finger hovering over the red button. "Send your Daddy after me if you want. If it makes you feel better, send your pit-bull mother and your creepy ass sisters too – they hate my guts anyway. Send them all. Send Godzilla, King Kong and North Korea while you're at it. Have a nice life Anita."

"This is your last warning. If you..."

Mike hit the red button.

"So long," he said, breathing a sigh of relief. He waited for her to try calling him again, but she didn't. Thank God, he thought. Still, even though he'd come through the hard part with Anita there was something uneasy sitting in the pit of Mike's stomach. It was a feeling. A feeling that he couldn't shake.

He whistled something improvised and happy as he drove, hoping that the sweet melody would make everything alright.

3

———

At last, Mike's attention was fully on the road. He leaned forward in the driver's seat, gripping the wheel as the headlights plowed two cylinders of yellowish light through the unusually potent darkness. Mike was beginning to feel like he'd strayed into an uncharted wasteland trapped in permanent night. There was nothing on either side of the road to give him some indication of where he was or where he was going to. There were only scattered silhouettes and shapes, all thinning out as time passed. He was nowhere. The lights of all the towns near and far, reminders of civilization, were gone. Even the markings on the road seemed transparent. Like they were fading away.

"Genius," Mike said. "I need some help getting home. Activate self-drive and Genius-Nav. Take me onto the Bronx River Parkway, heading south to Greenwich Street, Tribeca. Back home. Revert back to manual when we're on the parkway and give me two minutes notice before reverting."

Genius's voice, still the robotic default, was crisp and alert.

"Thank you Mike. Searching for Bronx River Parkway. Traveling south to New York City."

"Yeah," Mike said, still trying to shake the unease niggling his stomach. How could he have strayed off-route so quickly?

He stared at the oversized dash to the left of the wheel, waiting for the map display to come up and reveal his mistake. It was that damn conversation with Anita – it had distracted him. Thrown him off. He glanced outside and realized he was driving through a void. A landscape starved of scenery, reminiscent of the minds of some of the Hollywood executives he had to deal with on a regular basis.

"I'm sorry Mike. I cannot find Bronx River Parkway."

Mike scowled at the dash. "You're kidding man. I just left Scarsdale for God's sake. I'm hardly on the far side of the world, am I? Get your shit together Genius and take me back to New York City. I don't care if you have to sprout wings and fly there to get it done. Just do it. New York City."

A pause.

"I'm sorry Mike. I cannot find New York City. Would you like to try another destination?"

Mike hammered a fist off the steering wheel. "Another destination my ass. Are you telling me that New York City has disappeared off the face of the map just like that? It's thirty miles away at most for God's sake. What's going on? Is there something interfering with the GPS or what?"

"I'm sorry Mike. I do not understand the question."

"Forget it," Mike said. "Stay on manual and I'll find my own way home."

Mike kept his left hand on the wheel while the right tried to punch up the car's location on the map. But the GPS wouldn't show the map, which meant that Mike didn't have the first clue where he was. He tried his cell and the maps weren't working there either, no matter which app he opened up. Reception was sketchy at best, which was another weird addition to the night's proceedings. Had there been anyone around, he would've been forced to pull over and ask for directions. But this was a lonely road and seemingly in the middle of nowhere. There was no one out running or taking the dog for a walk. Mike couldn't remember the last time he'd seen another car on the road.

His face creased up into a frown. The dark, monotonous scenery continued to dominate the landscape, not even offering a left or right turn and the hope of getting off the road and onto another. There was only this; straight ahead and a black desert.

He tried to shoo away the panic clawing its way towards the surface of his mind.

"Easy man," he said. "You got this."

He could barely see three meters in front of the car. Mike brought his foot off the gas pedal a little, slowing the Genius down to around fifty miles per hour. At the same time, his inner voice told him to speed up, told him to get out like it had when he'd been walking out of Anita's house for the last time. It felt like he was sinking deep into the overwhelming quiet, broken only by the muted hum of the Genius skating over the two-lane blacktop.

Looking outside, he felt like he was making contact with something invisible, something with eyes that never left the car. Mike found himself thinking about all those hillbilly horror movies where the unsuspecting victims went off-route and found themselves knee-deep in cannibal country.

"Shut up," he said, scolding himself. "Think about something else."

His fingers tapped off the steering wheel. He tried singing to himself to lighten the mood – 'You Are the

Sunshine of My Life.' He looked at the dash. The map was still blank, leaving Mike cruising through No Man's Land. There were only the digital displays to look at – the speedometer, engine temperature and fuel gauge, all lit up in neon shades of green and red.

"Genius," Mike said. "Are you there?"

"Yes Mike. How can I help you this evening?"

"This silence is driving me crazy man. And since we don't know where the hell we are, I'd like some company for a while. Activate Passenger."

"Certainly Mike. Choose from your favorites – Who would you like to talk to this evening? Richard Pryor, Norma Jean Baker, Dick Gregory, Muhammad Ali, Barack Obama..."

Mike didn't need or want to hear the full list. "Let's go with Norma Jean. Be nice to talk to a woman that isn't throwing the kitchen sink at my ass."

"Activating Norma Jean Baker."

The whirring noise emanated from the speakers front, back and sides. A tinny click, another brief whirring and then a blinding camera-like flash. The flash lit up like a TV screen to reveal the image of Norma Jean Baker, head back, legs crossed and a relaxed expression on her exquisite face. The default setting inside Passenger had been for Norma's alter ego, Marilyn Monroe, but Mike had always preferred the pre-fame images he'd seen of the young Norma Jean. Maybe it was the happiness he'd seen in her eyes, or something close to happiness compared to the beautiful but broken eyes of the 'sex goddess'. With a little guidance and modification, Genius had made some alterations to Marilyn. Now she was Norma Jean again.

She was dressed in a casual white shirt with teal polka dots. Her reddish-brown hair was tied back, the makeup subtle and modest.

"What's up Mike?" she asked. She pointed at his chest, counting quietly to herself. "You're pushing a hundred and fifteen beats per minute. A hundred and eighteen. Wow, is everything okay?"

Mike felt a trickle of sweat on his neck. "My heartrate will keep going up if I know you're keeping count. Can you stop please?"

"Sorry. What's up?"

He shook his head. "Everything's up. I broke up with Anita and now I can't find my way back home. You ever seen a road as lifeless or as bleak as this one? I'm starting to think that the universe is trying to tell me something."

"Like what?"

"I'll let you know."

"Yeah, I heard the call with Anita," Norma Jean said, watching Mike and not the road. "So that's it? It's over?"

"It's over," Mike said. "Her temper was pushing double digits on the Richter Scale tonight. That was the last straw."

"She was no good for you anyway," Norma Jean said, electronic empathy in her blue eyes. "You guys were always fighting. What was it you always said? That damn temper of hers. You must have said that like a thousand times or something."

"Yeah, I know."

Mike stared through the windshield at a black desert of road, longing for something to reveal itself. An oasis of information, a nugget of promise, anything to let him know he was going in the right direction. That was all he wanted. That and a stiff drink.

"She was good for me," he said after a long silence. "After Tracey."

The light around Norma Jean's elbow flickered on and

off. The top of her head cut out and then switched back on again. "Heading back to the apartment?"

"Trying to," Mike said. "But GPS ain't picking up shit and I haven't seen a single sign for miles. Looks like I'm taking the scenic route without the scenery."

"Better lock the door when you get home," Norma Jean said, giggling. "Just in case Anita's dad comes looking for you."

Mike wore a half-smile. "You heard that?"

Norma Jean's voice was fading. "Oh yeah. You're in trouble now buster."

"I will NOT answer the phone or door for at least a week when I get out of this maze. That's a promise. Just in case Mr. Flaming Candy himself pays me a visit with a shotgun."

"Sounds...like...need...rest...and..."

"You're cutting out Norma Jean," Mike said. "Looks like Passenger isn't immune to whatever's going on around here either. Man, this place is weird and I'm talking X-Files on acid weird. I sure hope a big ass UFO isn't about to show up and kidnap my ass away to another galaxy. Wait a minute, on second thoughts..."

He glanced at the hologram.

"Thanks for listening Norma Jean, but without GPS I'd better keep my eyes on the road and work on getting back home."

She winked. "Call me. If the silence gets, you know, too much."

"You got it. Genius, turn off the VP."

Norma Jean Baker disappeared and Mike was alone again. He focused on the winding road that beckoned him forward, always promising something better just up ahead and never delivering. There were no houses, no distant lights and no sign of getting anywhere anytime soon. There was no blowing wind outside, no rain, moon or stars. There were the headlights and three meters of road, and that was it.

The bleak monotony was so powerful that Mike almost burst out laughing. "No wonder I don't know where I am. There's nothing to see. Nothing but..."

The car jerked suddenly on the road. Mike clamped both hands on the wheel, wondering if he'd ran into something that had jumped out in front of him. He hit the brakes but the Genius kept going, weaving aggressively from side to side as if trying to keep the heat in the rubber tires. And then it took off in a straight line. The engine screamed and shattered the silence. Mike stared at the speedometer in horror, watching the numbers go up. Sixty, sixty-five, seventy.

"Woah!" he cried out. He whacked the steering wheel as if trying to get someone's attention. "Genius. What are you doing? Cancel self-drive for God's sake. Abort. Abort."

The locks snapped shut, front and back. Mike felt the fear stirring inside him, a different fear that told him something was seriously wrong. This was no ordinary mechanical failure he was experiencing. Something was doing this. *Someone* was doing this. Sitting bolt upright in the seat, Mike tried to steer the car towards the side of the road but the wheel was rigid. It went about two inches either way before seizing up on him.

"ABORT! BRAKE! STOP!"

Seventy-five miles per hour, approaching a tight corner that looked like the entrance to a black hole.

"Stop goddammit!"

The car shuddered like it was about to angle up and take off. It careened around the corner at a terrific speed and the brake lights flared wildly at the back. There was a loud screech. The Genius cleared the turn with about an inch to spare, avoiding contact with whatever was behind the black wall that bordered the road.

"Help!" Mike yelled, hitting the wheel like he was trying to hammer it through the front dash. "Stop the car!"

The Genius was on a straight, approaching ninety miles per hour. Mike's sweaty hands clawed at the wheel even though it was clear he had precisely zero control over the car. *So who does have control?* Deeper, he thought. You're going deeper into this thing and there's nothing you can do about it. His body tensed up. Mike saw something – the beginning of a shape filling up the empty horizon. He leaned forward, still gripping the wheel like it meant something. Was that it? Was it over?

The horizon approached the lone vehicle. That's what it felt like to Mike, and not the other way around.

The outline of tall trees, tightly bunched together and surrounded by a light gray, simmering mist. More trees appearing on either side of the road, crowding the single-lane track that carried the Genius into a world of surreal woodland like something out of a fairy tale. The road, flat until now, began to steepen but despite this, Mike still felt that freefall floating sensation in his body like he was going back down on a rollercoaster.

Occasional spurts of color appeared in the floating mist – greens, reds and blues, as well as occasional flashes of silver and gold.

"Genius," Mike said. "Where am I? Where have you taken me and who's controlling the car? Can you hear me?"

No answer.

The Genius slowed to seventy miles per hour, enjoying another stretch of flat road. But even though the speed of the car was easing off, the track was still certain death if the

Genius kept going at this berserker speed. Sooner or later, the end would come. Slam into a wall of trees, another car, or turn over on a sharp bend. It was coming and there was nothing Mike could do about it. He was a prisoner inside the rogue vehicle and he could only sit there, watching through the window as the dark woods reeled him in.

4

"You sick twisted bitch!"

It was obvious – it was so damn obvious that Mike should've caught on as soon as the car started acting like it had a mind of its own. But it didn't have a mind of its own. It was Anita. She was, to use a technical term, mindfucking him.

Mike was sure of it because he'd read an article online, maybe two or three months ago, about a guy from Australia who'd pled guilty to stalking and controlling his girlfriend's Genius Car via his laptop and smartphone. This creep had downloaded and set up an online app that gave him control of around seventy percent of the car's features, including the stop and start functions, as well as (unbelievably) the ability to accelerate and decelerate. The stalker could also track his girlfriend's location at all times. The reason he could do all this? Because he'd bought the Genius Car as a gift for the poor woman. As purchaser, he had access to the VIN and that allowed him into the app that was capable of remotely controlling the car. Intended for emergencies, he'd used the app for stalking and terrorizing.

Mike recalled the story being all over Twitter, thinking that it would make a hell of a good movie. He didn't realize back then that he'd be starring in the sequel.

"Bitch," he said. "Evil bitch."

Anita had bought the Genius for Mike and as the buyer she had access to the VIN. Now she'd taken control of the car from the comfort of her armchair, treating both it and Mike like worn out toys she wanted to obliterate in the nastiest way possible. It was the only thing that made sense. Mike was both shocked and relieved at the same time when he made the connection. At least the car wasn't possessed Stephen King-style and it wasn't an inherent malfunction that couldn't be stopped. Come to think of it, Mike wasn't that surprised. Anita was capable of this, ensuring from the get-go that she had ultimate control over the Genius and thus Mike. With the app, she could track his whereabouts at all times and she could override his ability to drive home should the need ever arise. Like, if Mike ever broke up with her and she wanted to enact a particularly nasty revenge.

"Crazy," Mike said, shaking his head. "This is crazy."

He glanced at the door, at the dash, at the roof. Searching for anything unusual, anything suspicious – some hint of spyware that Anita had set up so she could sit back on the couch at home with a big bowl of popcorn and relish the terror on Mike's face as she remote controlled the car at breakneck speed along these narrow, winding roads that led nowhere. Way to take the power back.

Mike ran his fingers along the dash, probing the surface for anything abnormal. There had to be something that didn't belong there. He glanced at the speedometer, a set of numbers he had no control over. The digital display was wavering at seventy.

He pounded his fist off the steering wheel. "Can you hear me Anita? Are you watching me right now?"

He thumped his fist off the ceiling next.

"Stop it!" he yelled. "Stop it now before this becomes something you can't take back. You hear me? I'm going to die out here for Christ's sake – these roads are lethal. This isn't just my life you're screwing around with here Anita. It's yours, your sisters and your mom's too. You kill me and it's over for Flaming Candy and everything you guys have worked for over the years. Are you listening to me?"

Mike glanced out the passenger side window, his brow furrowed in a grid of creases. The dark woods, seemingly endless, was still closing in on the car. Tightening its grip, choking out the rest of the world.

"What the...?"

Mike resumed his frantic search for the spyware. Probably a pinhole camera or something he had zero chance of spotting in the dark. He envisioned a wobbly, tearstained Anita sitting on the couch in Scarsdale, gin and tonic in hand, laptop on lap, getting meaner and drunker by the second.

Secondhand drunk driving. That's how he was going to die.

Only in America.

"Now I know why you picked a Genius," Mike said, steering his attention away from the erratic speedometer. "I've had this car for three months. Three months! Tell me something Anita – have you been tracking me every time I've taken it out? You got a journal of my driving expeditions sitting on your bedside locker that you look over every night before turning out the light? Huh? You're crazy. You're fucking crazy."

Mike took his hands off the wheel, clenching both fists

so tight that he felt his nails cutting into his skin. He felt dizzy as the car began to speed up all over again. What if he needed to puke? Would she pull over for him? He scanned the dash and called Anita on the speed dial, hoping that a conversation would be enough to end this stupidity. The call rang out. With a groan, Mike grabbed his cellphone off the passenger seat and tried both Anita's cell and the Scarsdale landline. Nothing. He threw the phone back onto the seat, feeling the world collapsing underneath him.

"So now *you* don't want to talk?" he said. "Huh? You're letting me know that *you* don't want to talk to me. Oh my God. We're playing games, is that right? Childish games that end up with you killing my ass on these dead-end roads."

The tree-shaped silhouettes outside were a blur. Seemed like Anita was pushing the car towards ninety again.

Mike braced himself like a nervous flyer on the brink of takeoff. "So what now? You're going to run me off a cliff or something? Is that the plan?"

He looked outside. The trees *were* coming closer to the road and at the sight of them, Mike felt his dormant claustrophobia creeping towards the surface. He was as helpless as the day he'd been born. The doors were locked. He'd tried forcing them open, yanking on the metal handle with all his might, releasing the lever and then pulling again and again. Barging his shoulder against the door, knowing it was a waste of energy but doing it anyway because he couldn't stand being cooped up like this. He didn't care what speed the car was going – he'd dive out and take control of his own death. It was better than being trapped inside this cage on wheels at the mercy of a woman scorned.

It was hot. So damn hot. Mike felt like he was sitting underneath a magnifying glass in direct sunlight.

Eighty miles per hour.

Loud music exploded out of the Genius's speakers. It was the latest Flaming Candy single, 'Heartbreaker', and it was playing so loud that Mike felt his teeth rattle. The sugary pop song with high-pitched, chipmunk vocals was too much, especially at the intense volume it was playing now. The tinny treble scraped against the inside of Mike's head like a rake, while the bass felt like a caveman pounding a wooden club against his brain.

'Heartbreaker, heartbreaker,
crazy about you baby,
heartbreaker, heartbreaker,
thinking about you all the time, thinking now I'm going to lose
my mind.'

"Anita!" Mike roared over the wall of sound. Although he'd never said anything to his ex-girlfriend or her sisters for obvious reasons, he hated Flaming Candy's squeaky, fast-paced music with a passion. It was the musical equivalent of an epileptic fit and yet the kids loved it. "What the fuck are you doing? This isn't a video game for Christ's sake woman – slow down or you're going to crash into one of the trees. Is that what you want? Are you trying to scare me or kill me?"

He glanced at the speedometer. Ninety miles per hour.

"Oh Jesus," he said, fidgeting with the seat belt strap and making sure the metal tongue was clasped and secure in the buckle. "Okay, let's be reasonable here Anita. You've made your point and I hear you. I handled things badly tonight, I handled the whole thing very badly and for that I'm sorry. I'm an asshole. You want to talk? Let's talk. It's not over, you hear me? It's not over between us, oh Mary mother of God, what are you doing to me?"

He was about to die. This was it, this was the end and it was coming any moment now. Did he really want his last words to be begging words? Begging a crazy bitch not to murder him?

"LET ME OUTTA HERE!"

Mike felt like he was floating. Weightless. Trapped inside an International Space Station on wheels. That rollercoaster headrush was still there and so was the claustrophobia, everything running at full throttle. Boxed in, he hated being boxed in. Mike recalled how as a kid he'd always taken the stairs instead of the elevator in the apartment building he grew up in. Didn't matter that he was on the fifth floor, didn't matter how many flights of stairs he had to climb in order to avoid that mechanical coffin. He was walking. Sometimes though, if he was with his mom, he had to take the elevator at her insistence and those days well and truly sucked. He was sweating as soon as he stepped inside. The sight of those sliding doors closing over, that freaky-ass bump as the elevator began its ascent or descent. The stuff of nightmares. Then it was just a matter of praying. So far, the prayers had worked.

"What do you want me to say?" Mike asked, stabbing the brake with his foot over and over again. "Want me to tell you that I'm scared? Alright. I'm scared shitless. You want me to beg? I'm begging you now. You're hurling me down a single-track road at almost a hundred miles per hour and if something comes the other way, I'm dead and so is anyone unfortunate enough to be in the other car. If this car skids off the road, I'm most likely dead too. They'll trace this back to you Anita, you know that right? We've watched CSI together and those cats are smart. They'll figure this thing out in five minutes. You won't survive prison, I know that much. Flaming Candy will be history and your mom will be heartbroken at the death of her dream. Your sisters will never escape the shadow of what you're about to do either. Not when they look and sound exactly like you. Are you really going to throw it all away just because I broke up with you?"

He stared at the dash, waiting for Anita's call to come through. Hoping that at least one of the things he'd just said had made an impact. At the very least, Mike thought, let the car slow down.

"Override!" he yelled, pounding the roof with throbbing knuckles. "Override. Stop the car, stop the car! Slow down."

He could see tomorrow's headlines. Oscar-winning director killed by faulty Genius Car. That would lead to further ongoing discussion about Genius Cars, ethics, the many risks of self-drive and the irresponsibility of tech giants in the advanced automobile industry. Anita might even get away with it, despite Mike's insistence otherwise. Investigators would call it mechanical failure, a computer gone haywire and hey shit happens. Flaming Candy would go on tour as scheduled and Mike Harvey's legacy would fizzle out amidst a heated debate about technology. In the end he'd be a footnote, an afterthought in his own death. Occasionally they'd talk about his movies on Reddit, complaining about the direction he'd taken with those damn superhero movies instead of doing more things like his indie breakout, *Manhattan Hipsters*, the film that had delivered Mike his Oscar for its portrayal of black artists living in New York. They'd talk about how Mike killed off Brown Jaguar in his second comic book movie, the only colored character in that universe, and they'd say that in the end, he was just making movies to please the white man. They'd never know Mike's real strategy – that he was making those shitty movies in order to obtain more power and influence in Hollywood so he could bring in more of those high-quality black movies like *Manhattan Hipsters*. It was a long-term strategy and he believed in what he was doing. Only now that strategy was destined to go up in flames on a desolate backroad.

Sweat gushed down his face. The A/C was blasting out so much hot air that the car felt like the inside of a microwave oven.

"Anita. I can't breathe."

His head fell against the window. Still, the dark woods outside were endless. This was a blurry, formless shape and Mike felt like it was swallowing him alive. He couldn't see anything; there was no light in the distance, no colors, nothing. It felt like he'd driven off the end of the world and landed in single-track limbo.

"Anita..."

He sat up. The car was beginning to slow down. Mike watched, not daring to breathe as the numbers on the dash dipped from a hundred to ninety, from eighty to seventy and it lingered at sixty, which felt like crawling.

Mike was practically hugging the steering wheel. "Thank God."

The Genius was soon chugging along at thirty miles per hour. There was no sound out there. The woods, bathed in shades of gray and black, continued to move closer. Damn thing was moving, it had to be.

Mike had always hated the dark woods, especially at night. The Blair Witch had a lot to answer for but it wasn't just that old movie that creeped him out. The dark woods – this was where people who'd committed murder came, driving miles out of their way to bury dead bodies, the remains of which some dogwalker would stumble upon years in the future. But this was the worst he'd ever seen. These particular woods were like something out of an original fairy tale, the twisted and gruesome versions, long before they were watered down and made safe for children.

Mike tapped the dash.

"Genius, where am I? Where are we going? North? South? East? West? Can you give me anything?"

Genius didn't answer.

"Fuck you too."

Mike wrestled with the steering wheel, but it wouldn't budge. With a sigh of defeat, he fell back into the driver's seat, no longer the driver but a helpless, exhausted passenger. He stared dead-eyed through the windshield as the car continued to glide through the otherworldly landscape.

"Where are you taking me?" he asked. "Where are you taking me?"

5

___

Mike flinched as an explosion of light flooded the rearview mirror. A siren wailed three times and then stopped. Flashing blue and red lights blinked atop the roof of the other vehicle, a solitary beacon that told Mike he was in deep shit.

"Oh God."

His body shook. A river of cold sweat ran down his back, enough to drown in.

"No," he said. "Not the cops, not the cops for Christ's sake."

It wasn't just being black that made Mike wary of the cops. And it wasn't just because he didn't know where the hell he was or that the Genius had been speeding like a lunatic racecar along these roads that probably had a limit of sixty-five max. It was the fate of Eddie, his eldest brother. Eddie Harvey had only been seventeen when a routine stop in Jersey had escalated into the shooting incident that ended his life. Sure, there'd been a little weed in the car but it was a tiny amount intended for personal use. Eddie was no dealer, contrary to what they said in the newspapers. That narrative was bullshit, but ever since that day, Mike's mom and dad had been terrified that a similar fate would befall their youngest son who'd only been ten when his big brother died. Mike had inherited that fear of the law, even though his old man was a well-respected judge and was part of the machine that had failed Eddie.

Mike sat upright in the driver's seat, his rational mind attempting to soothe his fears, whispering a reminder that all cops weren't Cecil Proudfoot, the man who'd shot – *murdered* – his brother back in the nineties.

The sirens chirped again, letting Mike know that he was supposed to pull over. His slippery hands gripped the wheel, eyes glued to the mirror. He recognized the car as one of the regular traffic unit vehicles that patrolled around Scarsdale and its outskirts on a daily basis.

"Anita," Mike said, trying to talk like a ventriloquist and keep his mouth still. "You got what you wanted, alright? Happy now?"

The Genius *was* slowing down. It rolled to a stop at the side of the road, the tires crunching over ample layers of dirt and gravel. Mike breathed a sigh of relief, wiping the sweat off his brow and knowing that he was looking far from his best.

All that sweat, he thought. This guy's going to think I'm an addict.

"Anita," he said, keeping his voice to a whisper. "After everything I told you about Eddie, you get me pulled over by a cop in the middle of nowhere? Was that the plan all along? Thanks a lot."

The police car pulled in about a car's length behind the Genius, its blinding headlights like two forks in Mike's eyes. There was a long, excruciating delay before the driver's door opened. Mike's heart was thumping as he listened to the heavy footsteps getting closer.

"Easy," Mike whispered. "Take it easy. You'll get through this if you play it nice and cool."

He turned off the engine and wondered if that was a mistake. Like he was telling the cop that sure, he knew the drill. *I'se an old hand when it comes to this getting pulled over by the po-lice Mr. Bossman sir.* With a sigh, Mike lowered the window and saw a tall man, standing a few meters back from the car. Mike couldn't see the officer's face; it was cloaked in darkness, the features out of reach of the police car's headlights pointing from afar. Mike saw the badge though, pinned to the left side of cop's chest and gleaming proudly.

"Good evening officer," he said.

"Good evening sir," the cop said in a flat, colorless voice. "Do you know the reason I pulled you over tonight?"

Mike nodded, wearing a half-smile he hoped wasn't a smirk. "Umm, I might have been going a tad over the speed limit. That right?"

"A tad? Very good sir. Clocked you back there doing over a hundred miles per hour, barely even slowing down for the corners too. It's a miracle you're still alive. Why are you driving so fast this evening? Are you trying to kill yourself or some innocent family that might be driving in the other direction?"

Mike felt his insides clenching up.

"Okay," he said. "This is going to sound crazy officer but what I'm about to tell you is the truth."

"Uh-huh," the cop said. "Where have I heard that one before?"

Mike glanced at the tall silhouette with the cop badge.

That monotone voice – there was something familiar about it.

"I think my girlfriend, ex-girlfriend as of tonight, has taken control of my car. It's a Genius Car and this kind of thing has happened before in Australia – I'm not making it up Officer. I read about it in the news a couple of months ago. I think my girlfriend downloaded an app, that along with the VIN, gives her the ability to override the controls and mess around with the self-drive. In other words, she's very angry."

There was long pause.

"The car's yours?" the cop asked.

Mike peered at the shadowy figure, trying to make out the details of his face. He needed to see that face. Was the guy frowning? Was his expression neutral? Those eyes – what were they doing? "It's mine officer. I got the paperwork right here. You wanna see it?"

The cop tilted his head. "Are you alright sir? You seem anxious. Extremely nervous, one might say."

Mike thought that was a pretty dumb question all things considering. Anyone who'd been pulled over by the cops was entitled to be a little nervous about it. Especially a black man who'd been speeding through no fault of his own.

"Tough night," Mike said.

The officer leaned forward, his face coming close to the bubble of light. Mike glanced at him and his body shook all over again. Cecil Proudfoot. The cop who pulled the trigger, the cop who'd testified in court that Eddie had a gun in the car even though everyone who knew Eddie Harvey knew that was stone cold bullshit. Eddie couldn't even shoot a gun for God's sake. Most likely, Proudfoot, whose reputation in the force was far from spotless, had planted the weapon to save his own ass. And of course, he was still a free man.

The cop's angular features disappeared back into the shadows.

"You sure you're alright sir?"

"Fine," Mike said. He'd imagined it. There was no way in the world that was Cecil Proudfoot standing out there beside his car. No way. What were the chances of ever running into that asshole in a place like this? He was seeing things, hallucinating, and with everything that had happened so far tonight, who could blame his imagination for running away with itself?

The officer cracked his neck. "Say, aren't you that black director? The one that bagged an Oscar last year?"

Mike tried to smile. "Three years ago. But yeah, that's me. Mike Harvey, black director."

"Yeah," the cop said, still talking in a dreary monotone voice. "I thought you looked familiar." He scratched his chin and it sounded to Mike like he had sandpaper for stubble. "You're the one they keep saying, what was it again? What do they say about you? Oh yeah, you're the guy that sold out."

Mike braced himself.

"Started off with those handheld indie films," the cop said. "Didn't you? Black films about black people in New York, right? Black writers, black filmmakers, black painters, sitting around talking in cafes and la-di-da. Black history. Black lives matter. Cost you five dollars to make and made about five hundred million, right?"

That last part sounded particularly resentful.

"*Manhattan Hipsters*," Mike said. "That was the one that took off. And sure, it did alright at the bank, yeah."

The cop exhaled, long and hard.

"How'd you go from that artsy fartsy stuff to making

those trashy superhero movies? Jesus, didn't you direct the one where Brown Jaguar got nuked?"

"Guilty," Mike said.

"Black guy always dies, huh?" the cop said, laughing. And it *was* Proudfoot's laugh because Mike would never forget hearing it that day in court after the son of a bitch walked and was celebrating outside with his people. Celebrating while Eddie lay dead in a fresh grave. Mike's folks had taken him to court because his old man, bless his heart, believed that Mike would witness justice that day. No such luck. What Mike learned was that all his parents' good standing in the community didn't mean a damn thing and that Eddie Harvey would forever be remembered as a drug dealer.

No. That was crazy. The laugh – it didn't mean it was really Cecil Proudfoot standing out there on the road. Meters away from Mike's car, almost within touching distance. Mike was just having some kind of weird reaction to the getting pulled over thing. If the guy would step closer to the car and stay there for longer than a second, Mike would see that it wasn't Proudfoot. It was someone else. It *was* someone else.

"Anyway," the cop said, making no effort to step back into the light, "I guess that superhero stuff is where the big bucks are, right? Capes and tights, not preachy, job-shy blacks sitting around, smoking dope and talking about Malcolm X and *creative diversity*."

The cop kept talking in that flat, zombie voice. His lips, what little Mike could see of them, barely moved. "They said on one of those movie websites or forums or whatever the hell you call them, that and I quote, 'former indie darling Mike Harvey sold his soul for Mammon'. You hear that one?"

Mike sat up straight, his back drenched in sweat. "What's that officer?"

"Mammon," the cop said. "MA-MMON. Riches. Material wealth. They said that once you got a hold of the Oscar you stopped telling worthwhile stories and that it was all about the paycheck after that. Hell, there's nothing wrong with that if you ask me. Man gotta eat, right? Artistic integrity doesn't pay the bills."

Mike wasn't about to give the cop the reaction he wanted. Even though it felt like he'd been transported back in time to Mississippi in the 1930s.

"Oh right," he said. "Well, I'm still telling stories officer. They come in many shapes and sizes, you know how it is."

Mike turned towards the window, moving extra slowly so as not to spook the badge-wearing asshole. His voice remained in neutral. "Is all this really necessary officer? I think the point is that my ex-girlfriend is interfering with my ability to drive safely. I don't know how to override what she's done with the car. I don't even know where I am right now. Can you tell me?"

The cop stood tall, blending in with the trees in the background. "Hey Mike, I have a question for you. Is being black still problematic in Hollywood? Even nowadays?"

Mike's heart was drumming.

You're going to get through this.

"You'd be surprised officer," he said. "Being black is a trend to some people, you know what I mean? Sometimes it goes out of fashion, both with audiences and the powers-that-be who can greenlight a movie. You ask me why I made the big budget superhero movies? Well I'll tell you. Longevity. Versatility. It's about becoming known as a writer-director first, as opposed to a black writer-director. You don't hear much about *white* writer-directors, do you?"

"But you're the guy who killed off Brown Jaguar," the cop said. He sounded hurt, like one of the overzealous fanboys that Mike sometimes ran into at the big conventions. Usually, they were wearing Brown Jaguar costumes. "How could you? Don't you know what Brown Jaguar meant to people? To *your* people? I don't know much about versatility but that sort of decision can't be good for longevity."

The hair on Mike's arms was standing up. "Brown Jaguar's death had nothing to do with color. The story required that a sacrifice be made and..."

"Ahh yes," the cop said, raising his voice for the entire state to hear. "The sacrificial Negro. Damn, didn't think you'd play up to that particular trope Mike."

Mike felt like someone struggling to keep his head above water. But he was still there, still kicking. "Uh-huh."

"Say, you're not an Uncle Tom are you?"

"Excuse me officer?"

"You've forgotten your history," the cop declared. "You're hiding. Hiding from yourself. Looks to me like you wanna do a Michael Jackson and turn into a white man. Or a white woman in his case."

The cop laughed and it was as lifeless as his speaking voice.

Okay, Mike thought to himself. Stay cool. He's just a jealous, racist asshole, bored with his dead-end life and looking to lash out at someone doing well. Especially if that someone doing well happens to be black. Fuck him. They're everywhere, but it didn't change the fact that this one had Mike trapped in a vulnerable position. Just ride it out, Mike coached himself. Ride it out. This too shall pass.

"Officer," he said, "if you're going to book me for speeding, I'd prefer that we just get on..."

"Your brother died, didn't he?"

Mike felt another bead of cold sweat running down his back. "How do you know so much about me?"

He still couldn't make out the cop's expression. The tone however, was one of scorn.

"You're famous Mike. And when you're famous, everybody knows everything about you. That's the trade. That's the price you pay for bagging the best seat in the restaurant, the best seat on an airplane, you know? Yeah, Eddie Harvey. I remember that story well. Very well indeed. Killed by a cop in New Jersey about twenty-five years ago, wasn't it? Has it been longer than that? Was all over the news for about a week or two, I do remember that. Still, with all these race-related shootings nowadays poor Eddie probably wouldn't have got a look in. Never would have got his fifteen minutes of fame, would he?"

A long pause.

"I think," Mike said in a quiet voice, "that I'm uncomfortable with this conversation officer. With that said, I'm going to start filming on my phone. Just for peace of mind."

The cop's tone of voice never wavered. "That's fine. Go right ahead Mike. I want you to be comfortable."

Mike grabbed his cellphone off the passenger seat. He unlocked it with his thumb but when he tried to activate the camera, the phone blanked out on him as if out of juice. Mike frowned. The battery was never dead – he always made sure he had enough charge when he was out and about in case of emergencies. He slotted the phone onto the charger stand under the dash. Nothing happened. It showed no sign that it was charging.

"That's weird," Mike said.

The cop leaned forward again, the darkness following him like a puppy. "Having tech difficulties, huh? Maybe the engine needs to be running for it to charge up."

Mike shook his head. "Not in this car."

"That's too bad," the cop said, slipping back into the darkness. "Looks like you won't be making a movie after all."

Mike lifted the phone off the charger, tossing it back onto the passenger seat. He stared at it like it was a friend that had betrayed him.

"Alright," the cop said. "Now that we've gotten to know each other a little better, I've got something to say to you Mike. And you're going to damn well hear it."

Mike turned to the cop. "Hear what?"

"I don't like the way you treated my little girl tonight."

Mike felt like he'd been tasered. "Huh? What'd you say?"

"You heard what I said."

"Anita?" Mike said, his voice going up an octave. "Anita Gordon is *your* daughter?"

The shadow cop nodded. "That's right," he said. "Anita Gordon is my daughter."

Mike was surprised to discover that the dominant emotion he felt upon hearing this news was relief. It was like water running down a thirsty throat. If nothing else, it made sense of an extremely unpleasant encounter. It still sucked, but this wasn't a random incident without logic anymore. Anita was still fucking with his mind, only now she was doing it through her dad. Anita's old man was a regular Scarsdale traffic cop? So much for him living down south somewhere. No wonder she'd been so intent on bagging a house in the area, although she'd never said anything about a family connection in the area. Holy shit, Mike thought, trying to process everything. Ten out of ten for revenge tactics – first she sabotaged the car then, as promised, she sent her old man after Mike to play the role of racist cop and put the fear of God into him. Anita, knowing that Mike had a fear of being pulled over, was probably cracking open a bottle of champagne on the couch. Toasting a job well done.

"She's quite something," Mike said, shaking his head. "Your daughter."

The cop's face remained a mystery. "We look after our own around here. If you take my meaning."

"Around here you say? And where exactly is that officer?"

"You don't know where you are?"

"Haven't got a clue."

The cop made a sort of chuckling noise under his breath. Then he started walking back to his patrol car.

"You have yourself a good evening Mr. Harvey," he called out. "Word of advice – I'd watch that speedometer a little more closely on your way home. New York City cops aren't as tolerant with reckless drivers as I am."

Mike popped his head out the open window and watched the cop walking towards his car. "What? Wait a minute. I can't drive my car for God's sake. Anita has..."

"I think you'll find everything's operational," the cop said, not turning back. "Get moving now."

Mike's head slid back through the gap. With a sigh, he tested the steering wheel, turning it left and right and to his delight he found it responsive, fully back under his control. He turned the engine on and embraced the familiar hum of a fully-functioning Genius Car.

"Thank God."

Was Anita still spying on him? Watching? Listening? With any luck, she'd passed out in a puddle of gin but either way, Mike decided not to say anything to provoke her. She'd had her fun.

He looked in the rearview and the cop, who probably didn't look anything like Cecil Proudfoot in the cold light of day, was back in his patrol car with the engine coughing to a start. Mike pondered the idea of coming back up to Scarsdale in the morning to register a formal complaint at the station. That would make the smug shit choke on his coffee and doughnuts. No wonder the asshole had stayed out of the light and no wonder he hadn't given his name either. Still, it wouldn't be too hard to find him. Not if Mike really wanted to.

But deep down, he already knew he wasn't coming back. He wasn't going to make a complaint either. Mike couldn't be bothered with the hassle and if everything he'd gone through so far was the cost of cutting ties with Anita and her family, he'd suck it up. Life was too short.

He heard the growl of the police car cruising past the Genius. The headlights blinded him for a split second and then they were gone, traveling in what Mike assumed (and hoped) was a southerly direction. But Mike was in no hurry to follow. He'd sit behind the wheel for a few minutes and wait. He would only start driving when those bright taillights had been swallowed by the dark.

6

——————

Mike continued along the road, driving just below fifty miles per hour. Still no road signs anywhere, but he reminded himself that he couldn't be too far off the beaten track if Anita's dad had tailed him from Scarsdale. Something would reveal itself soon so instead of getting worried, he thought about home. About the bottle of sixteen-year-old Lagavulin waiting for him in the liquor cabinet. How many refills would it take to get over tonight?

Screw it, he was getting wasted. All he had to do was get home.

The Genius was still a moving dot surrounded by an ocean of dark woods on either side. Would it ever end? Where was the reassuring cluster of lights from distant towns and cities? This was New York State with a population of almost twenty million people and yet it might as well have been a ghost town. It had never felt this empty before, even if it was a little after midnight. How long had Mike been driving through this strange void now, waiting for the GPS to kick in and get him out of here?

Apart from Sprain Ridge Park in Yonkers, Mike wasn't

aware of anything like this on the map around this part of Upstate New York. Nothing this size anyway. The stooped black trees, with their long-arm branches and claw tips, skewered the gloom.

He knew one thing for certain – first thing in the morning he was taking the car back to Genius HQ on East 77th. He'd tell them something wasn't quite right and order a thorough service from top to bottom. With any luck, they'd find the spyware that Anita had installed and alert him to its location. After that, they'd most likely offer him a replacement although Mike wasn't sure he wanted any part of another Genius. Not after tonight.

He tapped the brakes, slowing the car down.

Something was out there. He could hear a noise in the distance.

Drums. He could hear drums. Mike leaned forward, pressing his chest against the wheel. His puzzled face inched towards the windshield and he stared outside, trying to see beyond the two pinpricks of yellow headlights.

Those drums. They made Mike feel like he was a long way from New York State and on the cusp of something else. Something exotic. The tempo quickened, as if the drummers were excited by the Genius's approach.

"What the fuck is going on now?" Mike asked.

He flinched as a dial lit up on the dash panel. The stereo icon blinked as the speakers crackled, sounding like a needle on vinyl sliding its way towards the groove. Music bled from the speakers: haunting piano chords, a lamenting trumpet and the familiar voice of Lady Day herself, Billie Holliday, singing about the strange fruit swinging on the southern trees.

Mike's eyes darted between the road and the dash. He could no longer find the words to express the growing dread he felt inside. Dread that hurt like a bellyache. He was falling – falling into something deep and unknown.

The drumming slowed down, soothed by this new melody from inside the car. The rhythm distorted and dragged, twisting itself beyond all recognition as it kept time with Lady Day and the somber song. Drums had never sounded so mournful.

Mike sat rigid behind the wheel. He had to blink when he saw a sign on the road, not believing it was anything other than a trick of the mind. Was it real? Was that a sign at long last, coming into view? Yes, it was. The metal pole holding up the sign was slightly crooked, leaning to the left in the same direction as the tight bend waiting directly behind it. Mike's foot kissed the brakes, slowing the Genius to a crawl as it began to slide around the curve. He read the sign. Two words, printed in capital letters.

THE AFRICANARIUM.

As soon as he read it, Lady Day's voice cut out and the music stopped. Outside, the drums began to speed up again.

Mike felt sick. He began to wonder if he was hallucinating all of this. Had Anita drugged him somehow during the course of the evening and in reality, was he lying slumped against the wheel of the car in her driveway, foaming at the mouth? Or maybe she'd knocked him out with one of her coffee cup missiles and he was sprawled out on the kitchen floor, dreaming up this nightmare. Cops and claustrophobia. The dark woods and Cecil Proudfoot – all of these jigsaw pieces that made up Mike's fears coming together in one place.

"It has to be a dream," he said.

The cellphone was ringing on the passenger seat. Mike stared at the phone like it was a live grenade that someone had tossed through the window. He picked it up, tentatively bringing the speaker to his ear.

"Yeah?"

"Hello again Mike."

It was Proudfoot. No, not Proudfoot – it was Anita's dad, Officer Smartass who'd pulled Mike over and toyed with him. Daddy fuckface, getting revenge on the guy who'd broken his little pop star's heart. Nonetheless, that dull voice sent a chill down Mike's spine. He didn't ever want to hear that voice again and yet there it was.

Okay, so Anita gave him your number. That works. Everything still works here and if it doesn't it's all a dream anyway.

"Listen man," Mike said, the phone pressed tight against his ear. "I'm sorry about Anita and everything that went down tonight, okay? I don't want any trouble. She's a great girl. This isn't about her. It's me. I just think we..."

"Mike..."

"What?"

"Relax," the cop said. "This isn't anything to worry about. You're in a movie. It's only a movie."

Proudfoot's voice (*not Proudfoot damn it*) was both a whisper and a deafening call from afar.

"What did you say?" Mike asked. "I'm in a...?"

"You're in a movie."

"What does that mean?"

"You're the movie guy, right? Think of this as being an old horror movie written by you. It's black and white, haven't you noticed? Look outside Mike, don't you see it?"

Mike glanced through the front and side windows. There was no color out there. He was driving through a world of pulsing shades, a monochrome landscape with only a single island of color left – the Genius and Mike sitting inside it. Proudfoot was right. It did look like he was traveling through the set of an old movie.

"What is this?" Mike asked, his voice scratched from all the shouting. "This isn't Anita's doing, is it? She's not sitting at home remote controlling the car and taking me wherever she wants me to go. Right? It's you – you're doing this."

"Didn't you see the sign?" Proudfoot said.

"I saw it."

The drums were reaching a feverish crescendo.

"The black guy always dies," Proudfoot said, the sentence tailing off with a cruel laugh. "Just like in those old horror movies from the 1930s, 1940s, you know what I mean? Black guy always dies, sooner rather than later. And guess what? In this movie, you're the sacrificial Negro."

"Fuck you," Mike said. "Fuck you whoever you are."

"You broke Anita's heart," Proudfoot said. "No one hurts my family and gets away with it. That's a rule of mine."

Mike gasped. "Gets away with it? Breaking up with someone is hardly crime of the century for God's sake."

He glanced in the mirror and screamed at the sight of his reflection. He dropped the phone like it was made of hot lava. It wasn't his face in the glass – his eyes were grotesque and swollen. His features had distorted into a caricature of the scaredy cat black character with the buggy eyes. The one from the old movies.

"JESUS!"

The car skidded to a stop in the middle of the road. Mike's body jerked forward in the seat and he began slapping himself on the face as if he was being attacked by a horde of wasps.

"No! No! No!"

He buried his head in his hands. His heart felt like it was thumping in his ears.

"No. You did NOT see that."

Eventually he lowered his hands. He approached the mirror in slow motion, his body trembling, seemingly on the brink of another panic attack. Mike saw the top of a head in the glass and thank God, it was his. He almost wept. *His head. His face.* At the same time, tinny-sounding laughter spilled out of the phone that he'd dropped on his lap.

Mike picked up the phone and the laughter stopped.

"Africanarium," he said. "What the hell's that supposed to be? Some kind of white supremacist theme park? What do you want from me man? All I want to do is go home for God's sake. Let me out of this, whatever *this* is. Proudfoot, are you still there?"

No answer.

Mike stared at the phone. "Hello? HELLO? Moth-erfucker!"

He tossed the phone onto the seat, pushed the driver's door open and hurried outside into the night. Mike gagged on the first lungful of air which smelled of decaying flesh. Like there was an open mass grave somewhere close. He slapped a hand over his mouth, staggered towards the side of the road and threw up until there was nothing left. He stayed like that, parked in a crouch for a few minutes where the road met the dark woods. Apart from the car, he was still the only speck of color to be seen in this strange place.

There was a sudden cracking noise above his head. Standing up and taking a step backwards, Mike stared towards a map of thick branches, gnarly and intertwined that seemed to lean unnaturally over the road. *Whoosh.* He saw the movement. Shadowy figures hanging from the trees, swinging from the lowest branches. Their coal black faces and sparkling white teeth seemed to float towards Mike.

They reached for him with arms that were little more than bones, eyes big and swollen with longing.

And then a voice.

Eddie's voice.

"Yo Mikeeeey!"

Mike's heart almost stopped. He was running back to the car before he knew it, almost tripping over his feet in the middle of the road. He slammed into the Genius like he was trying to tackle it and turn it over onto its side. As he leaned on the car for support, he glanced over his shoulder and saw nothing in the trees.

Now he knew for sure, there was something evil in those woods. And it was watching him.

Mike hurried back inside the car and punched up Anita's name on the dash. His hands were shaking. He chose video call and to his surprise, Anita answered immediately as if she'd been waiting for him. She was sitting at the kitchen table and there was no sign of the gin or champagne bottle that Mike had envisioned her cradling after his departure. She was still dressed in the same clothes, drinking nothing stronger than a mug of tea or coffee by the looks of it.

"Anita," Mike said, his voice trembling along with his hands. "Ever since I left your house it feels like I'm going crazy. What's happening to me?"

Anita wiped something from the corner of her eye. "Mike," she whispered. "I'm so sorry. I didn't..."

Her voice cracked.

"I'm sorry."

"This isn't a dream?" Mike asked, frantically scanning both sides of the road. He wanted to make sure nothing was slithering out of the dark woods, crawling over the asphalt and making its way towards the car.

Yo Mikeeey!

"No. It's not a dream."

"What is it then?" Mike asked. "What is this place? Do you have any idea what I just saw hanging off the trees out there? What I heard one of them say to me and who that someone sounded like?"

She nodded. "He's gone too far."

Mike couldn't think straight. "Who? Your dad? What's he doing to me? Tell me what's happening Anita because nothing makes sense anymore."

"You won't believe me if I tell you," she said. "At least, not yet."

The words scrambled in tight knots at the tip of Mike's tongue. "What the hell is going on?"

"I'm so sorry Mike."

He pressed a finger to his lips and continued to monitor back and forth between Anita and what was happening outside. "No more apologies," he whispered. "What's going on? Just tell me straight up, what the hell's going on?"

Anita burst into a flood of tears, burying her face in her hands. She tried to say something but it was clear she was in no state of mind to talk. After about ten seconds, she hung up, apologizing for what felt to Mike like the thousandth time.

He whacked his hand off the blank screen.

"Anita! Come back. Come back for God's sake!"

7

Mike didn't care what speed he drove at anymore. Not after what he'd seen swinging in the trees out there, not after hearing his brother's voice calling out to him like he'd done when they were kids. *The exact same way.* He wasn't quite doing eighty miles per hour but the Genius was traveling a lot faster than it should have on a road that wasn't much wider than the car itself and one full of hidden bends and other nasty surprises.

"It's the twenty first century asshole," Mike said, checking the rearview both for flashing lights and to make sure his eyes weren't buggy again. "Haven't you seen *Get Out*? The black guy does NOT always die."

The drums were persistent. They were still there, beckoning Mike forward. Didn't matter how far he drove along the road either – it didn't sound like he was getting any closer or further away from the beat.

"Genius," he said, trying to focus on things he could control. Or at least, maybe control. "We're going to make it work this time. Alright? We haven't vanished off the face of the earth so I'm going to say this loud and clear and I want your smart AI ass to listen good. Take. Me. Home."

The Navigator didn't respond. Instead, the lights of the Virtual Passenger flickered on and off.

"Not now Norma Jean," Mike said, his eyes still on the road. "I'm still trying to get home."

He heard a noise like a whip cracking inside the car. That wasn't normal. The VP light switched on and off, convulsing like the flame on a magic birthday candle that wouldn't blow out no matter how hard you tried. Mike was about to verbally shut Norma Jean down when he looked to his right and saw Eddie Harvey sitting in the passenger seat. Eddie was dressed in the same clothes he'd worn on the day he died – a black and white, long-sleeved t-shirt with 'Save Ferris' printed on the front in bold letters, dark jeans and white Adidas sneakers that were still brand-new more than twenty years later. Mike remembered those sneakers. He'd gotten a matching pair at the same time, or rather his mom bought him a pair, much to Eddie's embarrassment because Mike was always – *always* – trying to copy his big brother in terms of clothes and mannerisms. Eddie was sitting upright in the seat, staring at his little brother with eyes that didn't blink. A misty stream of blood trickled from the bullet wound in his chest – a red waterfall running down the lower half of Eddie's shirt and dissolving into thin air before it could connect with the car seat. Then the wound would start bleeding again, an endless loop of suffering that Eddie didn't seem to notice, such was his focus on little brother sitting beside him.

"Yo Mikeeey."

Mike's back slammed against the driver's seat as if a strongman was pulling him on a rope from behind. His body felt like the inside of a freezer.

He quickly pulled the Genius onto the side of the road.

"No," he said, staring at the windshield and not the presence in the passenger seat. "You're not here. You're not here."

Mike wouldn't say his name. Couldn't say it. There was no need anyway because it wasn't Eddie sitting beside him in the car. It was a projection.

"Yo Mikeeey."

Mike leaned forward, the car seat making a loud cracking noise that sounded like bones snapping. He pressed his head against the cold steering wheel, knowing that he couldn't abandon the car because this thing, this evil presence or whatever it was tormenting him, wanted Mike to go outside. Screw that, he thought. A Genius hologram was no more than a hologram. It might be able to scare the shit out of him, but that's all it could do. It couldn't hurt him. Not really. Not physically at least.

"Genius," Mike said. "*Please*. Take me to New York City. Take me to..."

He almost said his address but somehow revealing that information felt wrong with the thing beside him.

Mike lifted his head off the wheel. Okay, what now? Maybe if he kept driving the Eddie-thing would go away, especially if he didn't look at it. Didn't feed it with attention and most of all, fear. And yet, he could hear that raspy, labored breathing and it sounded so real. The scent of rotten flesh was coming through the A/C vents and it was starting to make Mike feel ill.

"Yo..."

"SHUT UP! I'M NOT LEAVING THE CAR EDDIE. NOW FUCK OFF!"

So much for ignoring it.

The Eddie-thing's response to Mike yelling at it was to start convulsing in the passenger seat like it was having a full-blown seizure. It turned its body towards Mike, shaking like a piece of human jelly. It reached for Mike and as Mike backed away, the Eddie-thing started decaying in front of his eyes – the body bloating, some kind of pink blood-foam leaking from the nose and mouth, the skin turning green then red, hair, nails and teeth falling out in rapid succession. Mike, his back pressed tight against the driver's door, was screaming. He tried to remind himself that VPs were holographic simulations. *Not real, not real.* They couldn't make physical contact and it would be over soon.

What remained of the Eddie-thing's arm came closer. Closer, closer, closer. Mike screamed when he felt cold, spider-like fingers brushing up against his arm and his body spasmed. So much for his theory about being safe. His arm shot out behind him, shoulders locking up as he searched frantically for the door handle. When he found it, he pulled the lever down but the door wouldn't budge.

"FUCKING OPEN!"

A whisper in his ear.

"Yo Mikeeey."

The Eddie-thing sounded excited now, warming up to the challenge of driving Mike insane with fear. It was still convulsing, still decomposing and by now it was a wet gooey version of Eddie that inched closer to the driver's seat as if it was coming over to take the wheel. Every move it made was accompanied by a wet squelching noise that sounded very real. Definitely not a simulation made by the car.

"Get the fuck away from me!" Mike screamed.

His shoulder rammed the door. He could smell that rotten stink of death filling up the car and it was jamming its way up his nostrils like a poisonous intruder. He felt dizzy. Weak. He couldn't breathe. Mike put all his weight behind the assault on the door, realizing now that the Genius, his sanctuary, had become another part of the prison. As he thrashed around in the seat, trying to release the door, his head thumped against the roof but he registered no pain from the impact.

The walls, roof and floor of the Genius were all closing in on him, just like his dead brother's damp and sinewy arm.

"AGGH!"

There was a loud snap as the lock finally released. As the door swung open, Mike toppled out of the Genius, his back hitting the hard surface of the road. He began crawling towards the edge of the road, desperate to put as much distance between himself and the Eddie-thing as he could. Everything was a blur as he scrambled over the asphalt. He picked himself up. He was on two feet now, wobbly but breathing cleaner air now he was out of the car. He ran off road, started climbing a steep hill and ignoring the faint warning in his head that told him he was running into the dark woods. But at that moment, it didn't matter. Anything was better than staying in the Genius. Anything at all.

He looked back once. Saw that the car was now black and white like everything else.

No going back, he thought.

Despite the adrenaline rush, the steep climb soon got the better of Mike's legs. He dropped to his knees on a bed of dry leaves. His lungs were on fire and he gasped for breath.

Mike looked at his hands, arms, legs and the clothes he had on. He was the only piece of color in a black and white world. An anomaly. A character from a modern film super-imposed upon the background of an old one.

"How is this possible?" he said, in between deep breaths.

He could still hear his brother laughing down there on the road. Laughing Eddie, that's what their old man used to call the eldest Harvey boy when they were kids. Eddie *was* quick to laugh – that was one of the few things that Mike was certain about when he remembered his brother nowadays. Truth be told, he remembered the laugh more than his brother's face. It was a happy memory and one that hadn't faded like so many other things.

That laugh wasn't a happy memory now. It sent a clear message over the road, up the hill and into the dark woods.

Don't come back Mikey. Don't ever come back to the car.

8

Mike walked uphill, ignoring the stabbing pain in his legs and the stitch in his side that reminded him of all the gym trips he'd passed on.

There were no lights visible on the higher ground. No blinking gold promise of a town in the distance offering a way out of this mess. There was only the neverending gloom of permanent dusk that lingered on the outskirts of this strange place. And the heat – it was so hot in the woods, a stifling tropical heat that encouraged languid movement and a lot of sweating. Mike felt like he was roaming around inside a giant predator's stomach, trying to outrun the horrors of digestion. Hydrochloric acid burned his eyes. A thick, wet and sticky mucous membrane pressed close against his face, covering his mouth and nostrils, making it hard to breathe.

Eventually the ascent leveled out and Mike emerged onto a flat stretch of clearing. He walked through the clearing, coming into a narrow corridor surrounded by a cluster of trees with knotted limbs. Although the flat terrain was welcome, Mike needed a rest. He had to think. Try to figure out what he was supposed to do now that he couldn't go back to the car.

Damn, he could hardly see a thing.

He leaned his back up against a tree, glancing over his shoulder. Maybe it was worth trying the car one more time, he thought, just to check. But even if Eddie, *not Eddie*, was gone, what was to stop him coming back a few miles down the road? It was pretty obvious that whatever had pulled Mike into this place had control of the Genius car and could do whatever it wanted. It was toying with him.

"To hell with that."

Mike's stomach lurched at the memory of those spidery fingers touching him. He doubled over, although nothing came out this time except a little spit. He wiped his chin dry and leaned back against the tree. His eyelids, heavy and worn out, began to close over. Now that he'd stopped moving, both mental and physical exhaustion were setting in.

A loud whooshing noise from above. Fast and sudden.

Mike felt something grab his right shoulder and he vaulted off the trunk like a marble from a slingshot, letting out a cry of terror. He turned to face the tree, backpedaling, his eyes darting from side to side, searching for a glimpse of whatever had made contact. A falling branch? A snake?

"Eddie?"

He stepped back a few paces and that's when he saw the shadow people hanging off the trees. There were so many of them, hundreds of bodies swaying in the breeze, doll-like and strangely peaceful. They reached for Mike, their dark eyes yearning. Their faces were uniformly forced at an angle. White teeth, the lips moving and whispering broken words that were unable to become fully formed because of the rope fastened tight around their necks.

Mike backed away, one step at a time. But something took over and before he knew it, he was running at full speed and doing so in an awkward crouch, hands over his head as if fending off an avalanche of dead arms and ice-cold fingers. He staggered through the gaps, trying not to run face-first into the silent army of tree trunks that seemed intent on blocking his progress. The stitch in his side was back. It was biting down hard. Felt like razor-sharp teeth gnawing relentlessly at his waist. Mike ignored it as best he could and kept moving.

Adrenaline could only carry him so far. Mike, on the brink of either passing out or a heart attack, took cover under a large tree with a wide, sprawling base and prominent roots that burrowed deep into the soil. He looked up, making sure there was no one swinging from the branches before dropping onto his knees, the weight of his upper body pressed against the trunk. His lungs clawed for oxygen. The air was thin, like he was at the top of Everest. The heat, more smothering than ever.

"Get me out of here," he groaned. "Someone get me out of here for God's sake."

His eyes remained on the long, crooked branches overhead. His short-sleeved polo shirt was soaked with sweat. His Levi jeans likewise.

"Take it easy man, don't lose it. Nice and easy, nice and easy. There has to be a way out of here. You'll find it, you're gonna find it."

He heard branches snapping.

Slow, deliberate footsteps approached his quiet place.

Mike held his breath, too paralyzed with fear and exhaustion to move. Even if he could get up, his legs wouldn't carry him far. What the hell was he about to face now? The thought of what might live in the dark woods wasn't a pleasant one. He stared into the void, trying to figure out the source of the disturbance.

Somebody walked out of the gloom. It was Anita. She approached Mike, whose back was still pushed tight against the robust trunk.

"Hi Mike," she said.

She was black and white like everything else in the dark woods.

Mike stared at her, waiting for the illusion to fizzle out. He wasn't sure if he was supposed to be happy to see her or terrified. "Anita," he said. His voice was thin and small. "Please tell me what's going on. Please, just tell me."

She kneeled down beside him on the organic residue that littered the ground. Anita's eyes were large and damp. "I'm so sorry Mike. This is all my fault."

"What?" Mike said. "What's all your fault? For God's sake Anita – what have you done to me? Where am I?"

"Me and my stupid temper," she said. "It's no excuse babe, but I can't control it. I literally can't hold it back sometimes. You know?"

"No," Mike said, vigorously shaking his head. "I don't know anything Anita. Not a goddamn thing."

She broke eye contact. "It's...it's in my blood."

Mike wiped the sweat off his brow. He couldn't keep his voice down, such was the onslaught of emotion trying to reach the surface. "What's in your blood? What are you talking about? Will you stop fucking around and tell me what happened? What happened after I left your house tonight Anita because ever since then I've been trapped in a living nightmare."

"He's so spiteful," Anita said, staring into the distance and seemingly talking to herself. "And he doesn't do things by half, that's for sure. I thought he was just going to scare you a little, you know?"

"Scare me a little?"

"I swear Mike. That's what I thought."

"Anita, where am I?"

"You're in the dark woods."

Mike checked the cluster of branches above his head, still wary of hands that wanted to come down and touch his face. "I can see that for Christ's sake. I can see it's dark and that it's the fucking woods. But look at me Anita – I'm the only thing that isn't black and white. Your old man said I was in a movie. What's that all about? What *are* the dark woods?"

"Your mind."

Mike felt like he'd been poked with a giant stick. "My...*what*? My mind?"

"Kind of," Anita said. She was barely able to look him in the eyes. "Put it this way – imagine your worst fears became a place. All your nightmares gathered together in one location, that sort of thing. Well, for you it's here."

Mike ran his hands over his scalding hot face. "How is this even possible?"

"Daddy knows everything about you. He knows about Eddie. Knows how you feel about cops and especially getting pulled over by cops. About dark woods, claustrophobia, and he knows that deep down you worry about amounting to nothing in life."

Mike screwed up his face. "Amounting to nothing?"

"You know what I mean," Anita said. "That part of you that thinks all your success was just a fluke and that maybe your luck's starting to run out in the movie world. It's true, isn't it Mike? You might look like a big deal to the average joe but on the inside you're just as scared as everyone else about not being good enough. About failure. About how other people see you. Maybe even more so, after what happened to Eddie and the way the media talked about him. Then there's all the criticism you've been getting hit with over the past couple of years about those superhero movies. You know what they say – that the cracks are starting to show. That Mike Harvey's on the slide."

"Cracks?" Mike said.

Anita pointed over Mike's shoulder. "Those people you saw, the ones hanging off the trees?"

"Yeah?"

"They were made to feel like nothing," Anita said. "Back in the day, people like that lived their lives in fear of the mob breaking into their houses in the dead of night. Taking them and their children away, despite the screaming and the pleading and the crying, and all because of the color of their skin."

"They don't hang black people from trees anymore," Mike said.

Anita nodded. "I know, but Daddy wants you to think that they do. More importantly, he wants you to feel it. He wants you to feel just like those people felt before they had their hands tied around their backs, before someone slipped the noose around their necks. From big movie guy to nothing – that's what Daddy wants."

"Those people weren't nothing," Mike said, glancing skyward. "The people who hung them, they were nothing."

"I know that," Anita said. "And you know that. Daddy knows that too but he doesn't care – it's about breaking you. That's the end goal."

"He wants to crush my spirit?" Mike asked. "Yeah, that much I gathered already."

"Yeah."

Mike looked at her. "Are you standing here? I mean, are you really standing here in front of me or am I imagining all of this?"

Anita's eyes roamed the surroundings. There was a long, penetrating silence before she spoke in a whisper. "I'm not really here. If I was, he'd know for sure. And if I stay too long, he'll definitely know for sure."

"Then how can you...how can I see you?"

She smiled. "I have, umm, certain powers. Let's put it that way. It comes with the territory, just like the temper and it's the same with Lindy and Roz. Everything flows through him and comes to us. His blood is our blood, whether we like it or not."

"Anita," Mike said, thinking back to the shadowy cop who'd pulled him over. The one who'd sounded a lot like Cecil Proudfoot. "Who is your dad?"

There was a nervous smile on Anita's black and white face. She looked like a starlet from an old movie, talking to Mike directly through the big screen. "C'mon babe. Do I have to spell it out for you?"

"Yeah," he said. "Spell it out for me."

She closed her eyes, tilting her head back like she was listening to the night. "You weren't seriously expecting horns and a pointy tail, were you?"

She opened her eyes, gauging Mike's reaction.

Mike's hands were clamped over his ears like a child that didn't want to hear it was time for bed. "I'm not listening to this. This is crazy talk man, it's crazy."

Anita sat down, cross-legged in front of him. "Makes sense though, doesn't it? When you consider everything that's happened."

"Nothing makes sense anymore," Mike said.

Anita rubbed something out of the corner of her eye.

"It's my fault. When you walked out on me tonight, I lost it. And then, once you'd driven off, I did something really stupid and something that can't be undone. I made contact. I made contact for the first time in a long time. It's not that hard for a blood relative to do, even though I'm like the daughter that doesn't call much. Especially compared to Lindy and Roz. Daddy's little girls for sure, much more appreciative of their family line, let's put it that way."

"Your sisters hate my guts," Mike said. "Do they know? About me being here?"

"They know. Expect to see them sooner or later. They're not going to miss an opportunity like this."

"Perfect."

Mike had heard more than enough to make his head swim. "Jesus Christ. What did you do? Did you organize a family Zoom call or something?"

Anita reached for Mike, then pulled away again as if she realized she couldn't touch him. "Something like that, yeah. Couldn't keep my mouth shut. Told them what an asshole you were tonight and how I wished more than anything that I could wipe that smug grin off your face."

"So the family are going to take care of that for you?" Mike said.

"I'm sorry."

"I can't believe what I'm hearing Anita," he said. "But how can I not believe it when all this is happening right before my eyes. You're the daughter of...how on Earth did *that* even happen?"

Anita sighed. "Mom."

"What do you mean?"

"You know Mom was the first singer in the family, right? She loved to sing but she never got much encouragement from her folks or anyone else in her immediate circle of friends and family. That's just the way it was. Get a job Martha, they said. Stop dreaming, get a job and be just like your sister and brother, live within a five miles radius of the family and make a life here with us. Make a life, that's a joke. They didn't understand the fire that drove her and how hard it drove her so Mom left home at seventeen, took the bus from Indiana to New York with three hundred dollars in her purse. Nothing else. She worked her ass off in the city, did everything right. But she didn't make it."

"Knowing Martha, I bet she took that well," Mike said.

Anita smiled. "She wasn't always the ball-buster she is now. From what I gather, she was a sweet kid who worked hard and never got the breaks. Luck is everything in show-business. Forget talent and hard work. Ten years passed since she'd left Indiana and still she was waiting tables in Queens and scraping by month to month to put food on the table and pay rent and bills. She fell into a major depression and although she beat it, she never lost her hunger for fame. If anything, she wanted it more than ever after the black dog cleared out of her mind. Fame was a way out. But by then she felt like she was too old, even though she was only thirty-two for God's sake. So, she decided that her kids would do what she couldn't. Not that she had any kids at that point, or even a boyfriend."

"So what happened?" Mike said. "Obviously something happened or we wouldn't be here."

Anita nodded. "It was like an obsession for her. Not like – it *was* an obsession. She planned it all out and everything that Flaming Candy became, everything we have, my mom, Martha Gordon, had it written down on pen and paper before me and my sisters were even born. Conceive, believe, achieve. You know how it goes. And this time around, she was willing to do whatever it took to get what she wanted.

Boy, was she willing. She did her research and started dabbling in what she labeled 'the dark arts'. She joined all kind of cults up and down the east coast, shitty ones at first but eventually she made the right connections. Slowly, she worked her way into a tight inner circle of the occult. Rituals, orgies, blood sacrifices – she did it all. And all for fame. All to feed the desire that still burned. She made contact with the dark side and I mean the *really* fucking dark side. A deal was struck. Just like the ones you hear about in books and movies."

"Let me guess," Mike said, not knowing whether to laugh or cry. "She sold her soul. Made a deal for fame and fortune. For your fame and fortune, and for Lindy and Roz's too."

"Yeah," Anita said. "A bargain as far as Mom was concerned."

Mike took his back off the trunk. His body ached like he'd run back-to-back marathons as a sprint. "That's a great story and I'm glad your mom finally got what she wanted out of life. But where does it leave me?"

"In deep shit," Anita said. "They're going to try and break you mentally. They're going to come up with all sorts of vile shit to destroy you and make you like the people in the trees. They, especially Lindy and Roz, thrive off mental torture. You see, Hell isn't dying Mike. It's being afraid all the time and if you're afraid long enough and hard enough then dying's the easy bit."

Mike kept his voice down. "What do I do?"

"You endure it," she said. "Don't give them what they want. And you sure as hell don't climb up into those trees and put a rope around your neck or you'll swing here in the dark forever like the rest of them."

Anita stood up. She backed away from the tree, starting

to fade out like a character at the end of a movie. "I gotta go Mike, I've been here too long."

"Why did you come here?" Mike said, getting back to his feet. His body cracked in protest.

"Because I'm sorry about what I've done to you," she said. "I never meant for it to go this far. Remember something, I'm part-human too. No one in the world is more frightened of what I am and what I'm capable of than myself."

"Lindy and Roz," Mike said. "Are they scared?"

Anita shook her head. "They're different. Watch out for them Mike."

She disappeared. The last thing she said was a whisper that came from far away.

"Don't give in Mike. You *can* win and you can get out of here and back into the regular world. But first, you have to survive."

9

The drums had stopped, but Mike took little comfort in the silence. Silence led to thought. If this place was indeed representative of his mind, as Anita had implied it was, then thought was a curse. Maybe even a death sentence.

Mike sat alone under the tree, hands tightly pressed against the sides of his head. Nothing could escape his mind, he thought. Nothing. *Don't think of anything.* But what if new thoughts weren't the real danger? Evil had already rummaged around in the basement of his experience – that much was clear. Perhaps it was too late to stop whatever was happening.

"Sunrise," Mike said, shivering despite the incessant heat. "If I can make it to sunrise then maybe this shithole will fizzle out like a nightmare." But he couldn't escape the thought that followed – what if there was no morning in this place? And if there was, what if the sun came up black and white?

"Oh fuck."

His throat was dry, aching for water. But what chance was there of finding water in a place like this? He was pretty sure that the roots of these trees absorbed evil. And what other life was there? There was only the stagnant stink of death and silence.

Mike leaned his head against the trunk. He felt his eyelids close over despite a feeble protest about the importance of staying awake. About the people in the trees. But Mike was exhausted and he was almost asleep when he heard the sound of roaring engines from nearby. The raucous disturbance pulled him back into the land of the living. He jumped to his feet, dizzy and off-balance. As the fog cleared, he rubbed his eyes and saw a wave of bright light gathering at the edge of the woodlands. Mike crept towards the light, walking for several minutes before he reached a steep incline that led down to where the woods met the road. He'd been that close to the road since coming into the dark woods? Felt like he'd been trapped in the heart of the woods, miles from anywhere. Or maybe things were still moving, like the trees that had moved closer to the car.

He dropped into a crouch, finding a gap in a nest of overgrown foliage.

Mike peered through the branches at a small convoy of vehicles. The convoy was slowing to a stop on the single-track lane, the same one that had brought the Genius Car from Scarsdale to here. Mike saw cars, vans, pickups and there was something that looked like a big yellow school bus at the back. It was so bright on the road that Mike didn't miss a thing; it was as if there was a set of giant stadium spotlights hanging overhead. He noticed the writing on the side of the nearest van. One word, etched in red letters, scrawled in paint that looked like it was still dripping.

AmeriKKKa.

"You've got to be shitting me," Mike said.

The engines began to cut out one by one. That's when

Mike became aware of the sound of dogs barking down there. The yapping was high-pitched. Frantic, unusually so. Mike couldn't see any dogs on the convoy or running around the road, at least not yet. What he did see were a bunch of raggedy orange tarps stretched across the back of several pickup, covering the beds entirely. Wave-like movement fluttered underneath the tarps, as if something was wriggling underneath.

"Don't matter what I do or think," Mike said, staring at the scene below. "This shit is coming for me no matter what. I've got no control over any of it."

His heart pounded as he glanced up at the trees. That's where they want me to go, he thought. Be a good Negro and know your place.

He recalled Anita's visit. Remembered her telling him that he could win and Mike knew that no matter what, he had to hang onto that thought even though it sounded like a pipe dream. A big fucking pipe dream. How the hell was he, a mere mortal, supposed to win if he was fighting against the...?

"Don't say it."

Mike flattened himself out on a bed of crisp leaves and branches. The good light down there meant he could see everything as clearly as if he was welcoming the newcomers in person. Mike wondered if the light was all from the vehicles or if the powers-that-be around here had thrown up a little extra so he could watch this arrival. He had the feeling that something wanted him to watch.

He saw one of the trucks hanging a U-turn, coming back on itself and pulling in at the side of the road nearest to the woods. It glided in slow motion. Attached to the trunk, a black and white Confederate flag flapped wildly in the breeze.

Doors began to open. The strangers stepped outside, setting foot on the jet-black asphalt.

Mike instinctively sank deeper into the long grass, burrowing his way into the soil. His eyes never left the road.

"Oh shit."

The shapes were immediately recognizable. The long robes, the familiar pointed hoods covering their heads. It was the Ku Klux Klan and yet it only took Mike a second to realize that it *wasn't* the Ku Klux Klan. Not really. It was some kind of monstrosity that resembled them, their bodies shaped exactly like the Klan uniform, their heads a grotesque imitation of the tall, conical-shaped hood with the back flap and rounded corners. Slits for eyes. The glossy satin surface of the robes wasn't part of their clothing, it was their skin.

"This?" Mike whispered. "This is in my head?"

The Klan monsters gathered in the middle of the road. Looked to Mike like the beginnings of a group huddle as they bunched tightly together, their cloak-like bodies jerking occasionally like someone was dishing out electric shocks. They roared with excitement and it sounded like the hissing screech of a prehistoric bird.

Mike could even see their long, sharp teeth. Wall to wall canines.

"Fuck me."

There was a loud clicking noise as the Klan creatures began communicating with one another. Mike didn't know what language they were talking or whether it even was a language, but it wasn't human. That much was for sure. Whatever it was, it was bird-like and concise.

Some of the monsters approached the back of the trucks. Working in unison, they peeled back the orange tarps that covered the bed and the pack of dogs underneath, sensing freedom, became more excited. The corners of the tarp were lifted. The barking intensified and Mike felt like he was going to throw up, even though there was nothing left to get rid of.

The tarps were discarded at the side of the road. There was more click-talk from the Klan and the beasts, obeying the commands of their masters, leaped over the side of the bed and landed on all fours on the road.

Mike strained his eyes, trying to get a better look at what was down there. It was obvious right from the get-go, when the beasts raised themselves off all fours, that these weren't dogs. They straightened up, extending their limbs into a confident, bipedal stance. They were human, sort of. They had long grasping arms, claw-like fingers that reached for the dark woods and what was in there. Thick, rope-like leashes were attached to spiked collars around their necks. Their masters maintained a tight grip on the collars, holding the dog-men back, at least for the moment.

"Jesus."

Mike wriggled forward a few inches. He saw something else and his jaw dropped, leaving his mouth a gaping hole.

The human dogs were wearing blackface. Blackface, holy shit. They were white people covered in dark paint just like actors from old movies whose faces had been darkened with shoe polish or greasepaint, with enlarged lips painted around their mouths. Blackface dogs. Mike watched as their noses twitched, taking in the scent of...what? Of Mike? Some of them frothed at the mouth, pulling at the ropes almost to the point of choking themselves unconscious.

Mike was dizzy with terror and confusion. It felt as if some unnatural tide was taking him closer to the nightmarish scene down there on the road. The dry blades of grass under his body was an army of little daggers puncturing his skin.

He watched as one of the Klan monsters marched up and down the line of blackface dogs, shoving something against the nose of the frenzied pack members. The object glowed, in bright color, the only thing in color apart from Mike hiding up there on the hill.

"No way," he whispered.

It was an Oscar. His Oscar. They were sniffing his damn award to get the scent.

Run you fucking idiot. What are you still doing here watching this for? Get up and run. Run for your life goddammit.

Mike felt his cellphone vibrating in his pocket. There was a jolt of terror as he frantically tried to claw the phone out and silence it, even though there was no way the creatures on the road could have heard it. He hammered his thumb off the green button three times before it stopped buzzing.

He stared at the phone, eyes wide with terror. What was it even doing there in his pocket in the first place? He'd left it in the car, hadn't he? It wasn't like he'd stopped to grab it during his encounter with the Eddie-thing. Especially not when the Eddie-thing had been sitting on it.

Proudfoot's monotone voice squirmed through the earpiece. "Are you there, Mike?"

Mike brought the phone towards his ear without letting it get too close. He didn't know what was going to jump out of that speaker. "Yeah, I'm here."

"Aren't you relieved?"

Mike's hand was shaking. He couldn't stop thinking about who he was talking to on the other end of the line. *What* he was talking to. It wasn't just a racist traffic cop and it wasn't Eddie's killer even though the voice sounded exactly like Proudfoot's. That voice, that dull *boring* voice. How could it be? Was he really talking to the...?

"I said, aren't you relieved?"

"Relieved?" Mike said, still watching the road down below. The Klan monsters were slapping each other on their hood-heads like footballers riling their teammates up for the big game ahead. They were screeching and clicking. The dogs drooled with anticipation and pulled on the collar ropes. "Relieved about what?"

"That it isn't you up there swinging off the trees," Proudfoot said. "That the color of your skin won't get you lynched anymore. Then again, what about Eddie? How insensitive of me – I guess there are still ways to get lynched that don't involve a rope. We don't live in enlightened times after all, do we?"

Mike glanced over his shoulder. The shadow people were hanging off the branches again. Hundreds of them, maybe thousands in total and even though their features were lost in the dark, Mike could feel their eyes all over him.

"You're fucking sick man," he said, knowing only too well that it wasn't a man he was talking to.

"Be happy," Proudfoot said. "You should be happy. Mike Harvey did well in life. He didn't grow up to be just another worthless nigger. Did he? You made your parents proud, not like your brother, the drug-dealing hoodlum, the good-for-nothing, the wannabe ghetto rat and whatever else the newspapers called Eddie. The one who brought shame on the family, shame on Papa Judge and Mama Scientist. But not you Mike. Mike matters, Mike is worthwhile, he means something to people. To all people, but to black people especially. He's a symbol of hope and it'd be terrible if something bad was to happen to change all that, wouldn't it? The shame he'd bring down on his family. The shame he'd bring down on his black brothers and sisters around the world."

The corpses on the trees moaned. Sounded like they were dying all over again.

"Fuck you," Mike said, watching those poor bastards wriggling in the air. A few of them kicked their legs like they'd been freshly strung up and weren't all the way dead yet. "I don't care who you are, I'm not scared of you."

"You're not?"

"No."

A pause.

"How fast can you run Mike?"

"Huh?"

"I hope you're a fast runner," Proudfoot said. "Because those things coming after you are fast – very fast and they're terribly destructive too. I fear for anyone that gets in their way. It isn't going to be pretty. I can tell you that."

The line went dead.

"Fuck you too," Mike said.

He let the phone slip out of his fingers. As he got back to his feet, Mike caught sight of something moving in between a cluster of low-hanging branches to his left. Peering out from behind the gnarly wooden limbs was a young woman's face. The face looked at Mike without expression. When he saw the long blonde hair, Mike's heart leapt with joy and he hurried over in that direction.

"Anita?"

Silence.

"Anita, is that you?"

Mike stopped dead. The differences between Anita and her sister Lindy were subtle to say the least, but if he got close enough, he could spot them well enough by now.

Lindy's forehead was a little wider. Her eyes rounder. But it was the cruel smile, that's what gave it away most of all.

Lindy was standing in bright color, a light unto herself. Roz Gordon was there too, positioned just a few paces behind her sister. Roz was similar in size and shape to the other Gordon girls and like Eddie Harvey a long time ago, Roz was always laughing. But Roz's laughter, unlike Eddie's, was rarely good-natured.

She was laughing now. Laughing and pointing at Mike like a kid who'd seen something funny across the street.

Mike blinked. When he looked over that way again, the sisters were gone.

He didn't doubt that he'd seen them. Anita told him that her sisters were in the dark woods and that they'd be coming after him. Mike hadn't doubted it either. This was just a warm-up, Act One, Scene One, just the girls letting Mike know that they were close.

He walked back over to the crest of the incline. Down on the road, the blackface dogs were back on all fours, slapping their hands (or was it paws?) off the unnaturally smooth asphalt surface, pulling on their leashes as if they were trying to flee from an erupting volcano. It was a miracle they could breathe, such was the pressure they were putting on the rope collars.

The Klan monsters were looking up at Mike. All of them. They knew exactly where he was, had probably known all along, and with a final screeching roar that came straight from Hell, the handlers slipped the ropes off their dogs' necks and released them into the dark woods.

10

————

There was a *pop-pop-pop* noise like fireworks. Like the beginning of a giant celebration was underway. The drums were back too, pounding like claps of thunder, each beat keeping pace with the frantic, runaway rhythm of Mike's heart as he fled for his life.

He could hear the blackface dogs barking behind him. Mike didn't look back. He didn't want to see those monstrous creatures as they reached the crest of the hill and emerged onto the flats behind him. He didn't want to see them sprinting on all fours, foaming at the mouth like a pack of human Cujos. He could hear them coming. Even over the fireworks and drums, he could hear their heavy feet trampling over fallen sticks and other debris that littered the floor of the dark woods.

Mike pumped his arms and legs, fear oiling the rust in his weary joints. He slalomed through the gaps in the trees, aware of a soft thudding noise all around him. The noise kept coming. Sounded like giant apples falling off the trees and hitting the ground beside him.

He glanced over his shoulder.

The dead were falling. They dropped from the trees like stones from a great height, landing on all fours and then rising to their full height, arms stretching out to the sides like they were unwrapping their bodies from a lifetime of bondage. They remained a part of the black and white landscape, blending in with the scenery like people who belonged in old photographs and in another time. With a tight noose still fastened around their necks, the dead began to run alongside Mike. They ran with their heads tilted to the side. Tongues protruding. Dead men, women, boys and girls. They ran like the wind.

The barking inside the dark woods got louder. Same with the fireworks. The drums were building up to an impossible speed.

Mike had to get out. There had to be a way out of this mess, even if this mess was a smorgasbord of horrors concocted in his own mind. He had to get out before his heart exploded or his legs crumbled and left him at the mercy of the monsters that lived here and chased his scent.

He gasped as his foot slipped on something soft like mud. Mike skated along for about two meters, then his left leg shot high in the air like he was about to attempt the world's worst backflip. He felt something – *someone* – grab his arm, secure a tight grip and stop his fall. Mike remained upright, cleared the mud patch and was back running at speed again on solid ground. He looked to his right but couldn't pick out his savior from the pack of shadows running alongside him.

Mike Harvey was no athlete but the thought of what would happen to him if he stopped moving was far worse than the thought of a heart attack.

He heard the hiss-roar of the Klan monsters, somewhere in between the howling and the barking and the fireworks and the drums. The dark woods were a cacophony of evil noise, each layer piled on top of the other to create a horrific symphony. It was the sound of insanity.

"C'mon!" he yelled, trying to push himself even harder. He was his own coach. His own lifeline.

Running wasn't easy. There were obstacles everywhere – dead tree stumps, rocks, small boulders and living trunks that revealed themselves at the last moment. Mike swerved and skipped over these on legs as heavy as cast iron weights. He was running on reserve energy but the hardest thing was that there was no end in sight. What was he running to? Where was the light at the end of the tunnel?

"Yo Mikeeey!"

One of the dead veered to the left so that he could run directly alongside Mike. The familiar presence in the 'Save Ferris' shirt edged closer, shoulders brushing up tight against his little brother. Mike squirmed at the sensation, at how soft and slushy his brother's shoulders were. He felt like he was running alongside a ticking bomb. He could still hear that wet squelching noise, the sound of his brother's body liquifying.

Somehow Mike was able to push the pace, like a seasoned distance runner on the final lap around the track. There was a head-splitting scream. He looked over his shoulder and saw that the blackface dogs had caught up with some of the shadow runners at the back of the fleeing group. The dogs leaped on the runners' backs, wrapped their long, sinewy arms around the tilted necks and viciously tugged on the noose, choking the dead with raw strength and a look of hate on their polished faces. Mike winced at the gagging sound of the shadow people fighting for air. How could that be? The dead were dead, weren't they? How could they die all over again? Mike couldn't take his eyes off the struggle, even though he knew he should've been concentrating on his own escape. After a brief tussle, the blackface dogs wrestled the dead to the ground and sank their sharp teeth into the bruised necks. It was feeding time. They were starving vampires and the blood flowed like a river, and it did so in bright color.

The dogs that didn't stop to feed tore through the dark woods, mostly pushing the shadow people out of the way. The Klan monsters were now visible in the distance, lighting massive fires and letting the flames devour everything in their path. Everything went up in flames, as if the monsters wanted to leave no trace of their presence. The drums kept drumming. The bodies, the trees, everything was ablaze. Mike could smell the putrid odor of rotting flesh, adding to the scent of decay that had been there from the start.

He coughed, fighting for clean air that was getting harder to find. He ran with everything he had. A sea of blood and fire was closing the gap behind him and he could feel it on the brink of smothering him. The fire was as dazzlingly orange as the blood was red. Black smoke, twirling in slow motion, ascended towards the sky that hung empty and lifeless over the dark woods.

There was a loud snarl at Mike's back. He felt the earth shake under his feet, as if being split open by a rampaging monster that dwelled underground.

One of the blackface dogs, a tall emaciated figure with protruding ribs and dog-like ears, chased after him. It was ahead of the pack, on two legs, its greasepainted skin dripping blood. The black eyes bulged with hunger and the sharp fangs, as red as the blood on its skin, were fully exposed.

Mike could feel its breath on the back of his neck. A foul

gust of air from the bowels of Hell. He cried out as a razor-sharp claw scraped along his shoulder, piercing the skin and trailing down his back as if drawing a straight line. It felt like a blowtorch tattooing his flesh. He shook off the contact and kept running. But there was no doubt that Mike was slowing down and meanwhile the dogs were getting stronger and faster. The gasoline in their veins was limitless evil.

Eventually, Mike's legs folded and he hit the ground, which felt like a slab of concrete. He instinctively flipped onto his back while the blackface dog leader, back on all fours, crawled towards him, primed to pounce like a wildcat.

"Fuck you!" Mike screamed. "Get away from me."

It leaped through the air but Mike rolled to the side, his body sliding out of reach of its hideous jaws. He felt himself tipping over the edge of a dip in the land. He was tumbling down a steep, jagged slope, hitting rocks and branches all the way, and seconds later his body slammed into the remains of a mangled tree stump. Before he had time to process the damage, there was a thudding noise behind Mike. He jerked onto his side and saw that the dog leader was only a few feet away. It began to crawl over the carcass of another ancient tree, licking its enlarged lips as it closed the gap on its prey.

"Get away!" Mike yelled. His voice was a pathetic whimper. He crawled backwards, pushing himself over the harsh terrain that seemed intent on slowing him down. He noticed movement on the path at the top of the slope. The other dogs were there, scurrying down the incline and falling in behind the pack leader. They gathered in the narrow corridor littered by dead stumps. There were at least thirty of them, all closing in on the scent of that gold statue.

Mike slowed down further. He had nothing left to give.

This wasn't a nightmare because no nightmare could

ever feel so real. As he sat on his backside waiting to die, Mike's life began to flash before his eyes like a home movie – fuzzy, grainy and poorly lit footage with faded color. He saw his parents, his contribution to humanity which felt slight to say the least, relationships, good deeds and bad deeds, and all the things he'd never do and places he'd never see. What would Mike's death here look like in the world of the living? Would his body turn up somewhere in that realm, floating off-shore, bloated and foul? Or would there be no body at all, his death destined to remain a mystery and a subject speculated over on conspiracy theory websites for decades to come?

Mike's eyes turned to the empty sky. He didn't want to look at them as they walked him down. Maybe he'd get lucky and die of exhaustion in the next second or two, go out in the comparative bliss of a massive heart attack or stroke. That way he'd feel nothing of their teeth sinking into his flesh.

He closed his eyes and waited for that first jolt of pain. The feeling of being eaten alive. He waited and waited and it didn't come. It felt like an eternity passed before Mike began to feel lightheaded and he wondered if this was dying at last, blacking out and thank God, experiencing nothing of the attack.

Death wasn't so bad. It felt like falling.

And then he heard something – a strange sound that didn't belong in the horrific place that he'd just been.

It was a woman. She was giggling.

11

Mike opened his eyes. He gasped out loud and frantically swatted at thin air, fending off the attack of the blackface dogs. Nothing. The dogs weren't there. They were gone and so too were the Klan monsters. There was no raging fire or river of blood, no drums, no fireworks, no shadow people and no corpses littering the floor.

He was dripping sweat, still covered in the dirt of the woodland floor. Still exhausted, but no longer in the dark woods.

Mike sat bolt upright, his eyes devouring the surroundings. Trying to make sense of things. He was back in Anita's house, looking straight onto the kitchen – the table, chairs, the countertop, pictures on the wall and the Flaming Candy calendar pinned to the fridge with Flaming Candy magnets. Anita's kitchen. This *was* Anita's kitchen in the house in Scarsdale – there was no doubt about that.

"It *was* a dream," Mike whispered. "Holy shit, just a crazy trip."

He climbed back to his feet, plagued by aches and pains. The pain was real – that was a concern, but maybe a fall had knocked him out and that was all he was feeling. Right? Maybe?

"It was a dream."

As he steadied himself, Mike became aware of a presence in the room. Two people were standing alongside him. One on either side, hovering at Mike's shoulders.

His heart sank. "Oh shit."

It wasn't over. Not by a long shot.

Lindy Gordon was standing to his left. Roz Gordon, to the right. Mike glanced warily at the two sisters. They were perfectly still and yet closing the gap between themselves and Mike, seemingly with no effort. Their matching white dresses trailed at their backs like cloaks. Their blonde, blue-eyed angelic smiles, no matter how pronounced, couldn't hide the loathing they felt for him. They did a good job of holding up their squeaky-clean family image for the cameras but in private, Lindy and Roz had always reminded Mike of adult versions of the girls from *The Shining*.

Come and play with us Mikey. Forever and ever and ever.

"Hi Mike," Lindy said. She was exactly like Anita in both voice and appearance, but her eyes were an Arctic wilderness. Mike was certain that if someone were to cut Lindy Gordon open on a slab, rocks and boulders would spill out instead of organs.

"What's going on now?" Mike asked in a blunt tone. "I'm getting pretty sick of this trippy-ass, torture shit."

"You don't know what's going on?" Roz said, glancing at her sister as if Mike was the school dumbass they were teasing in the corridor. "You *really* don't know?"

Mike reached out, pushing his palms against a massive slab of glass in front of him. There was no way past the glass. It was cold, like a sheet of smooth ice, and a barrier that stood in between him and Anita's kitchen on the other side. He looked through to the other side. The kitchen was empty, recessed ceiling lights throwing down a pale glow that maintained the moody ambience that Anita liked around the house. The broken plates and cups on the floor from earlier were gone.

"Why are we here?" Mike asked.

He felt like he was standing in a laboratory looking into the room where the experiments took place. There was even a faint hum in the background, like machinery sleeping and it added to the industrial coldness of the moment.

The Gordon sisters watched Mike. Their eyes widened as if he was something gross crawling along the dinner table.

"Wait for it," Lindy said. "It's coming. Any second now."

Mike heard the sound of car tires crunching over gravel in the distance. Headlights flooded the kitchen, a yellowish wave sweeping across the tiled walls. A car door slamming shut. Then another. This was followed by the thud of heavy footsteps approaching the house. Angry voices jostled for supremacy. The front door opened. A moment later, two people stormed into the kitchen, one of them throwing down a set of car keys onto the table as if trying to break them into a thousand pieces.

It was Anita and Mike.

"You've gotta be kidding me," Mike said, leaning his face against the glass. "What sort of new mindfuckery is this?"

Anita, her face bright red with anger as it had been earlier that night, walked over to the dining table. She spun around to face the other Mike who was standing beside the sink. They continued the argument that had already taken place. *It had already taken place!* Anita accused the other Mike of flirting with the waitress and he responded with a denial and then she started throwing plates and cups at him. Mike watched it all from the other side of the glass. He felt numb, wondering how something so stupid, an argument about nothing, had sent him down this Twilight Zone path he'd traveled tonight. Watching it now, he realized he could have handled the situation better. He could have shut it down. Kept his cool better. But then again, he'd been looking for a way to end the relationship. He couldn't pretend otherwise and tonight he'd seen and taken the opportunity when it presented itself.

Mike looked at the Gordon sisters. "What's the point of this? I was there when it happened the first time, remember?"

Lindy's eyes blinked slowly. "Just keep watching Mike. You haven't seen everything yet."

Mike sighed and turned back to the kitchen. He was still breathing heavy, trying to recover from the chase in the woods that had nearly killed him. The claw wound in his back stung like a bitch. He could feel the Gordon sisters watching him, feeding off his reaction as he took in the argument in Anita's kitchen. They wanted to see him break down piece by piece, so much so that he'd go back into the dark woods with a rope around his neck. Mike would give them no such pleasure. And why would he? He'd seen this shit already, lived through it as a participant. Watching it over again wasn't exactly going to drive him to suicide.

"Here it comes," Lindy said, her eyes lighting up.

There was a lull next door. The other Mike began to walk slowly away from the kitchen table, doing a lap of the room while Anita stayed put, weeping over his alleged flirting and stabbing a fork into the kitchen table. Mike didn't remember her crying. Not like that. And he didn't remember doing that lap either. He'd stayed put by the sink for the whole thing.

"What the…?"

The other Mike walked towards the viewing screen. He placed his head against the glass and stared at Mike, or at least appeared to be staring at Mike. What was he looking at – a regular kitchen wall? A framed photograph? Or could he see them in there? Their heads were merely inches apart and both Mikes could have been looking in a giant mirror. They stood there for almost a minute, eyeball to eyeball. In total silence. Eventually, the other Mike backed away and as he did, he winked as if to let them know he was in on the joke.

"The fuck?" Mike said, turning to the sisters.

"Brace yourself," Roz said, fighting back the laughter. "You don't want to miss this next part."

The other Mike took a deep breath, his nostrils twitching, chest expanding. He glared at Mike, cracked his knuckles and then spun around.

"BITCH, I'VE HAD JUST ABOUT ENOUGH OF YOUR SHIT TONIGHT!"

He stormed across the kitchen. Charging towards a wide-eyed Anita.

The other Mike grabbed Anita by the wrist and pulled her with such force that she bodysurfed across the kitchen table. Anita screamed, begging for him to let go. The other Mike dragged her off the table, legs kicking furiously. He threw her down onto the floor with brute force and when she tried to get up, Mike leaned over and punched her square in the jaw. There was a cracking noise as she fell backwards, curling up into a ball, screaming at the other Mike over the tears, begging him to stop.

Mike threw his body at the glass window, pounding the screen with both fists. "Leave her alone! Leave her alone you piece of shit! I'll fucking kill you."

Roz was doubled over behind him, unable to stem the tide of laughter. "It's you Mike. You're calling yourself a piece of shit!"

Mike paid no attention to her. He continued to hammer at the glass with everything he had. "LEAVE HER ALONE!"

The other Mike didn't leave Anita alone. And when he didn't, Mike continued to hurl his body off the screen, pummeling with his fists, kicking the glass with the flat of his shoes. There was no way through. The barrier was solid. Mike took a step back, looking past the gleeful sisters, wondering if there was another way into the kitchen. Nothing. The room they were in was shrouded in darkness and Mike knew that, no matter how hard he tried to find a way out, he was trapped in yet another nightmare. Of course there was no exit, at least not one that he had any control over.

"Anita!" he yelled, his voice cracking.

Lindy and Roz watched, feeding on Mike's desperation like a fire gorging on oxygen.

Eventually, the other Mike grabbed the keys off the table and stormed out of the kitchen, blood dripping off his knuckles. Mike stared at Anita, her body twitching on the kitchen floor, lying in a puddle of blood. The front door slammed shut. The car headlights lit up the kitchen wall again as the Genius roared down the driveway.

Mike's hands were clasped on top of his head. Anita was crawling over the floor, trying to make it to the kitchen door. She was crying, begging for help.

The lights began to dim and the kitchen fizzled out into nothingness. Mike felt like passing out, such was the weight in his heart.

"You evil fucking bitches," he said, staring at the dark screen. "Evil. Pure evil."

The sisters glided closer and a cold breeze filled the room.

"Wait till the press find out what you did tonight," Lindy said. "Wait till they find out what the great Mike Harvey did to America's sweetheart in her own home. You saw it too. He beat her senseless, to a bloody pulp. And then what? What became of Mike after that?"

"He became just another criminal in the family," Roz said. "Just like the drug dealer, Eddie."

Mike shook his head. "I'm not falling for this bullshit. I know exactly what you're trying to do and you can both fuck off."

"This *is* happening Mike," Lindy said. "What you saw in there – that happened in the world of the living. Think of it like a reconstruction. We reconstructed tonight's argument and made the outcome a little spicier. A little bloodier."

Roz leaned into Mike's ear. Mike felt her warm breath on his skin. "This is happening. This is how we're going to destroy you."

Lindy began to circle Mike slowly. Still gliding, moving without a sound. "You're in here with us," she said, "and the people you just saw are in New York."

Mike pointed at the glass. "Who was that guy?"

"I would've thought that much was obvious," Lindy said. "That guy was you."

"No, he's not me. *I'm* me."

Lindy clicked her fingers. The glass window, no longer a blank canvas, lit up once more like the screen in a movie theater, spitting out a collage of fast-moving images – Mike's double, blood still dripping off his knuckles, walking out of the dark woods, making his way towards a narrow road with no scenery on either side for miles and beyond. The double walking to Mike's car with a cruel smile on his face. The

Genius driving on a normal road, passing a sign that pointed towards New York City. The double getting out of the car and walking into Mike's apartment building in Tribeca. Then it was daylight and the double was in cuffs, being led out onto the street by police officers, surrounded by an onslaught of flashing cameras and microphones stabbing at his face. A large crowd had gathered on the street, watching as the cops led the double towards a waiting car. The crowd spat in the double's face. They yelled the word 'monster' over and over again in a frenzied chant. They held large banners over their heads that said 'HANG HIM.'

The image-train slowed down and began to cloud over. Then it faded into darkness. The glass was just glass and neither Mike's double nor Anita's kitchen were visible on the other side. There was only Mike and the Gordon sisters standing in a cold, shapeless room.

"That's gotta hurt," Lindy said. "How did that make you feel Mike, seeing your future laid out like that?"

"Did it hurt?" Roz asked. "In what way did it hurt?"

Mike tried to maintain a poker face. "I know what you're trying to do. And it won't work."

"Don't look so worried," Lindy said, her constant circling coming to a stop. "You won't miss out on all the excitement, I promise. You see, me and Roz have a plan. That last clip you saw a second ago was your double getting arrested for the assault on our sister. Now we're going to keep him in there right up until that point but after that happens, we're going to pull him out and put you back into the world of the living. Cool, huh? We're going to drop you off in New York right after the shit hits the fan. His fate, that'll become your fate. His punishment, your punishment."

"Tricks," Mike said. "Two stupid little girls playing stupid little games. That's all this is. None of this shit means anything. Right? What happened to those Ku Klux Klan things and their fucked-up dogs back there in the woods? Huh? Gone, just like your double and all the other scams you and your fucked up family are trying to sell. I know what's going on here. You're trying to break me. You want me to quit, to climb up a tree and put a rope around my neck. But I will never yield to this bullshit, never."

Roz stared at Mike's face like she was cramming for an exam on his wrinkles. "Oh yeah," she said. "The hunters and their dogs. Seems like Daddy's getting impatient in his old age. That was his idea you see, but let's be honest, they were a bit underwhelming. Weren't they Mike? Daddy's busy you see. He'd be happy to end this thing quick but that's not nearly enough punishment as far as we're concerned. A quick death? No, that's not how it's going to be. So we intervened."

"We know for sure," Lindy said, "that when Daddy sees our alternate plan for you, he'll be proud of us. We've put a lot of thought into this tonight you know. Avenging your sister's broken heart is hard work."

Mike laughed. "You're crazy. You really think anyone will believe that I did that to Anita? I've never had so much as a parking ticket before."

"They'll believe it," Roz said with a wicked grin. Mike noticed the braces clamped to her teeth which made her look even younger than her sisters. "And don't pretend like we haven't hit the sweet spot Mikey boy. We know you better than you think. Your self-esteem is bound up in material success and how others perceive you. Your reputation is so important to you. You want to be *someone* like your mommy and daddy with their nice jobs. You want them to be proud of you and you fear losing all of that and so much more. You fear being invisible, failure and poverty.

You fear becoming just another nigger like your brother Eddie."

"Eddie's going to look like a saint compared to you," Lindy said in a cold, metallic voice. "Unless..."

Mike glared at her. "Unless what?"

Lindy smiled and that was a rare treat Mike could have done without. It was like seeing a hungry crocodile up close. "Unless you do what we tell you. Because there *is* another way out of this mess, one with no shame for the Harvey family, no scandal and no bringing up all those unpleasant memories of Eddie."

"Oh yeah?" Mike said. "And what exactly do you want me to do?"

"Quit," Roz said, leaning in and putting her lips on his neck. Mike flinched. Roz's lips felt like two little icebergs. "Quit."

"Join the others," Lindy said. "Go willingly into the trees and we'll bring the other Mike back here and your reputation will stay intact. But you have to go willingly."

"Dying's great for your career," Roz said, perking up as if a lightbulb had just switched on over her head. "There's no better marketing plan in the world. Didn't the suits in Hollywood ever tell you that? I'm surprised they didn't tell you that."

Mike listened to the industrial hum in the background. Behind that, he was sure he could hear the faint sound of drumming.

"I know exactly how this thing plays out," he said in a quiet voice. "I go to the trees and you leave the imposter in New York anyway so that your Scooby-Doo plan goes ahead. I'll be dead in here and that woman-beating version of Mike Harvey lives to bring shame on me and my family's reputation. And you two girls, you get to watch it happen from the comfort of your mansions."

"No," Lindy said, shaking her head. "That's not how this works. You do what we ask and we'll do what we promise. And we do promise Mike."

"Do it," Roz whispered. "Kill yourself. Give in for the love of your Jesus, it's only going to get so much harder."

Mike felt the anger swelling up inside him. All things considered, he'd done a pretty good job of holding back so far but this time he couldn't stop it.

"Go to Hell!" he yelled. He pushed both sisters backwards at the same time and it felt good. "And give me some space you creepy ass bitches. I can't breathe in here. Now listen up and listen up good. What happened tonight was between me and Anita and it's none of your goddamn business. You got that little witch girls? We had a fight, we broke up and that's that. It happens. I didn't beat the shit out of her like your Frankenstein's monster back there so keep pushing me all you want. I won't break. I won't put a rope around my neck and give you the satisfaction of a job well done. You hear that? I will NOT break."

The sisters edged away slowly. Staring at Mike like he was a sewage leak on the bathroom floor.

"You'll break," Lindy said.

He shook his head. "I won't."

"You'll break," Roz said.

"Go fuck yourself. Both of you."

"You're going to suffer for this," Lindy said. "You'll become the most hated man in America, I promise. Your career and reputation will go down the toilet and of course, you'll watch your parents' mental and physical breakdown which we'll help speed along of course from the comfort of our mansions. Any way we can."

"Any way we can," Roz said.

Lindy halted her retreat. "Last chance Mike. Before this thing starts getting really ugly. You don't dump our sister and get away with it."

"Don't give me that bullshit," Mike said. "You don't give a shit about Anita. You heard that my torture party was going down tonight and you wet your little knickers with excitement. Now get the fuck outta here."

"Big mistake Mike," Lindy said, her voice trailing off.

He closed his eyes and heard the drums calling.

He waited.

Lightheadedness came and it was a relief. And then he was falling.

12

———

Mike was back in the dark woods.

He was sitting underneath a large monochrome tree, opening his eyes as if waking up from a short nap. A little groggy, his joints heavy and stiff. There were no Klan monsters or blackface dogs waiting to welcome him back into this version of his private Hell. There were no dead bodies scattered across the glum landscape and no one swinging from the trees either, reaching down, trying to touch him. It felt like he was truly alone.

Mike inhaled the wet earthy aroma that usually followed a rain shower. It was the first time that the dark woods hadn't reeked of death. Something else was different too. He could hear a noise.

Running water. More of a trickle than a run but what-ever, it was water and it was as sweet to Mike as the siren's song was to the desperate sailor. No, that couldn't be right. Water? Here? He scolded himself for daring to believe it. He was imagining it, wasn't he? Then again, was he still capable of imagining good things in a place like this? His mind felt like it had been reduced to a plaything for others, all his hidden fears mined like diamond ore and used against him.

But he was thirsty. He had to find out if that water was for real.

Mike winced as he climbed back to his feet. He was trapped in the body of a hundred-year-old man, a hardcore smoker who never took his vitamins. He listened, waiting for the illusory sound of water to pass. It didn't and that encouraged Mike to follow the sound. He plodded over the hard earth like someone walking underwater. A few minutes later, the dark woods led him onto a gentle downhill slope as if it understood the aches and pains that crisscrossed his body. As if it was showing him mercy.

He found the stream at the foot of the slope. It was narrow and slight, but undoubtedly real. The water flowed bright blue against the colorless woods, a living thing that existed in defiance of a dead place.

Mike wanted to cry. It was beautiful and as he staggered over and dropped to his knees beside it, a teardrop slipped from the corner of his eye and plummeted into the stream. He cupped his hands and shoveled the water down his throat. It was cold. Pure. Clean. Bliss. All the organs and tissues in his body began to stir, as did a little of Mike's shattered spirit that up until then, had felt like a puppy's chew toy.

He threw water over his face and that's when he heard branches snapping at his back. Whoever was there, they were close.

Mike raised his hands without thinking about it. Some fights you can't win.

"Alright. You got me man. Nice job sneaking up on my…"

"Hey Mike," he heard Anita say.

Mike wiped his chin dry and scrambled back to his feet.

He turned around and saw Anita standing a couple of meters back, still black and white, still a little fuzzy around the edges. But that didn't matter. He was overjoyed to see her, even if she was the spitting image of her demonic sisters.

She pointed at the stream. "Drink as much as you want. The water's safe, I promise."

"I hope so," Mike said. "I just drank half of it."

He smiled.

"You put it there, didn't you? With your spooky magic powers."

Anita assessed her handiwork, a snake-shaped oasis winding its way through the vast enormity of the woods. "Not bad, huh? I figured it's the least I could do, seeing as how it's my fault you're stuck in this limbo shithole with my family."

Mike wanted to hold her but he knew he couldn't. "I saw something terrible," he said. "Lindy and Roz, they got a hold of my ass and showed me..."

"That wasn't me," Anita said, cutting in. "Just like it wasn't you beating the crap out of me either. They're just fucking with you like I said they would."

"Thank God," Mike said. "That was horrible. I don't ever want to see anything like that ever again. Not ever."

Anita wasn't smiling. "Thing is Mike..."

"What?"

She took a deep breath. "The double's real, okay? He might not be you but he's real and what Lindy and Roz told you about sending him into the world of the living, that's real too. You need to take that very seriously. Once the shit hits the fan in New York, they'll drop you back into the heat. Just like they said they would."

Mike felt like he'd been sucker punched in the guts.

"Your sisters are evil," he said. "If the double does his thing and gets my ass arrested it'll kill my folks. It'll kill them Anita. You didn't see what Eddie's death did to them but I did and I can still remember it all these years later. The aftermath of the trial, what people said about him. My folks are too old to withstand that sort of heat again. They'll break, I know they will."

Anita looked like she'd swallowed a piece of glass. "I know."

"Lindy and Roz, they can do all this?" Mike asked. "They can *really* do it? Send that fake ass version of me out into the world?"

"Yeah."

"What else can you and your sisters do Anita?"

She shrugged. "We can do lots of things Mike. It's in our blood and once you discover the power that's always been there, it's hard to resist. I can almost understand why Lindy and Roz turned out to be so fucked up in the head. It's seductive, you know? We can dominate people's emotions, manipulate the weather, master all kinds of spells and rituals."

"Witches," Mike said. "You guys really are witches, right?"

"I suppose. It's not a word we ever use."

"And all of this comes from your father's power?" Mike asked.

"Yeah."

Mike nodded in the direction of the stream. "Won't he know you did that? That you built this stream for me?"

"It's possible," Anita said. "But I did it anyway."

"Why?"

"You know why."

Mike was desperate to go over to Anita and collapse in

her arms. He longed for that warm feeling of sinking inside her again. Even after everything that had happened it was clear that there was still something between them. Something strong. Why else would she put herself at risk like she had?

Anita lowered her head. "I may act like it sometimes, but I'm not a monster. Not like my sisters, not like Daddy. And I know that the chain of events I set off tonight is a thousand times worse than anything you ever did to me. Shit, you weren't even trying to be mean breaking up with me, not like I was by calling Daddy and the family together and screaming like a baby because my feelings were hurt. I screwed up, but that's why I'm here. I think I can get you out of this."

"I'm frightened to ask," Mike said.

Anita's eyes roamed the dark woods. Looked like she was making sure they were alone. "I'm willing to give you a chance Mike. That's if you're willing to take it."

"A chance?" Mike said.

"A chance to get out."

"And what exactly does a chance look like around here?"

"You need to break the spell," Anita said. "The one that Lindy and Roz conjured up tonight. Forget about the Ku Klux Klan bullshit – it's my sisters that will hurt you the most. I can't interfere with their magic directly – that's not how it works in this family with blood ties and all. That means you'll have to do the dirty work Mike. But if you stop the double, that version of reality that my sisters want will never happen."

"Won't they know you've helped me?" Mike asked.

"Maybe. I don't care. You know us, right? That sisters forever thing is just an act for the fans. It's bullshit. Lindy and Roz aren't doing this for me – they're doing it because they hate your guts."

"But there's two of them," Mike said. "Two versus one. Doesn't that make it harder for you to, you know, intervene or whatever?"

Anita shook her head. "The firstborn is always strongest."

"Firstborn? I didn't know you were the firstborn."

"By thirteen and a half minutes," she said, laughing quietly. "Thirteen and a half minutes of bliss before Lindy popped her big fat head out of Mom's hole and ruined everything." She laughed again. "Listen to me babe, I can give you a fighting chance but that's all I can give you. You'll have to do most of the work and like I said, it's dirty work. This guy, your double, he's on his way to New York now, to your apartment."

The thought sent a cold chill down Mike's spine. That monster walking into his home, taking ownership of his identity and effectively rendering the real Mike as non-existent. "He's on his way? Holy shit. Alright, say he gets there ahead of me – people will buy it?"

Anita was dead serious. "They'll buy it because he *is* Mike Harvey. Look babe, I get it. It sucks having other people that look like you, move like you, talk like you and sing like you. Imagine having two of them, everywhere and all the fucking time. It sucks, take it from me. But your mom and dad won't be able to tell the difference if this guy walks up and kisses them on the cheek. If you don't want to be the intruder in your own life, you have to kill him. Shit, he's even driving down there in a Genius Car with the same license plates as yours. Stop his clock Mike. Do it before he sets foot in the building you call home because if you don't, it becomes *his* home. And you'll come straight back here. That's how this shit works."

"Fuck," Mike said, feeling lightheaded again. "Let me get this straight. I have to drive back to New York and kill someone tonight?"

"You're not killing anyone," Anita said. "It's just a spell, remember that. You're breaking a spell."

"How? How do I get out of here for a start?"

Anita pointed over his shoulder, past the stream and towards a dimly lit corridor that ran as straight as an arrow through a mob of densely packed trees. "Keep going downhill. Follow the light and it'll take you back to the road."

Mike nodded. "Okay, that seems easy enough. But what about the double? What am I supposed to do to him?"

Anita checked that the coast was clear again. Then she stretched out her left arm and uncurled her fingers to reveal a small, exotic-looking dagger resting in her palm. The dagger was in full color, unlike Anita. The silver blade was thin and it glittered like fresh snow in the sun. The blade was attached to a gold and black leopard print handle that made it look, to Mike's untrained eyes at least, like something that had been lifted out of a thrift store.

"That little thing?"

"Take it," she said. "Quickly."

She slid the dagger into Mike's hand and it felt like she'd just handed him a sheet of ice. There was no weight to it at all.

"Looks more like a letter opener," Mike said, sounding unimpressed.

Anita wasn't in the mood for jokes. "That *letter opener* holds more power than you could possibly imagine. Don't fuck around with it Mike, you have no idea." She eyed the blade warily. "All you need to know is that it's capable of overpowering the spell. Use it wisely babe. And do what needs to be done, kill that double and break the spell before he sets foot in your home."

"I have to kill him," Mike said robotically, staring at the blade. "Kill."

"You're only breaking the spell Mike. Don't think of the spell like it's a regular person. It isn't. Got it?"

"Got it."

Anita pointed at the corridor of light. "Drive back to New York. Do this and you'll stay out of the dark woods forever."

Mike wanted to say something. To tell her that he still loved her and that he was grateful for all her help.

He opened his mouth, but Anita pressed a finger to her lips. "There's no time. Go."

13

____

It didn't take Mike long to find the road.

He followed Anita's dimly lit path, walking with the sound of running water in his ears. It was downhill all the way, a welcome break from the cruel and vicious landscape that he'd encountered so far. No more steep climbs to torture his sagging legs. No more racially-fueled nightmare scenarios from the darkest corners of his imagination. The shadow people in the trees were gone too. It was a simple, even hopeful walk back to the car and in the end, less than ten minutes in total from the stream to the Genius.

The road was different. As he stood beside the car, fingers touching the door handle, Mike saw sparkling orange lights on the horizon. Civilization, no more blackout. This was a regular road in the world of the living and there was even something up ahead that looked like a sign – directions to the parkway with any luck.

Mike glanced over his shoulder. The dark woods were gone and it was like they'd never been there. There was a sea of lights that told him he wasn't alone anymore. Overhead, stars blinked through the gaps in the clouds, complimented by a whisper of moonlight trickling down onto the quiet road.

"Oh God," Mike said.

His body fell against the car door, overcome with the beauty of it all. Even the air felt cleaner. Less malicious.

"C'mon man. You got no time for this."

He opened the door and flopped into the driver's seat. His body sounded like knuckles cracking.

"Jesus."

Mike pushed the starter and the engine purred to life, soft and smooth like nothing had happened. He checked the dash. Navigator, working fine. The route map display was fully functioning too, waiting for instructions. The blue pin on the map told Mike that he was only a mile southeast of Scarsdale, a short drive from Anita's house. Jesus, he thought. One mile. That's how far I've traveled? He noticed his cellphone in the passenger seat where he'd left it. Whatever device he'd been talking to Proudfoot on in the dark woods, it hadn't been his phone.

"Get your shit together," Mike said, glancing at his exhausted face in the mirror. Anything besides driving at this point was a waste of time, especially when he had the other Mike Harvey to catch up with.

The clock said it was three o'clock in the morning. How many hours had passed since he'd left Anita's house, fleeing her wrath and that samurai sword? He couldn't quite grasp the details. Everything was still a swirling fog in Mike's brain and he wondered if this was what it was like waking up from a coma, trying to figure out what year it was. Okay, it wasn't that bad. Couldn't be that bad, could it?

He placed Anita's knife on the passenger seat. Again, Mike marveled at its size and delicacy. It was such a tiny, fragile-looking weapon. The word 'weapon' even sounded like a stretch. It was nothing short of puny and yet there was something unnerving about the *letter opener* now sitting there beside his cellphone. Anita hadn't been comfortable around it. Mike had noticed that much. The last thing she'd told Mike before fading out was that he could only use the dagger once and that he had to make it count. It was a one and done thing. The power inside the blade, whatever that was, would be expelled after contact with the double. If Mike lived through this nightmare, what was he supposed to do with it then? Keep it as a souvenir? Throw it in the trash? Take it to a thrift store?

"One thing at a time," he said, steering the car off the side of the road.

He drove towards the distant lights. The world opened up and less than a minute into the journey he saw signs for the Bronx River Parkway. Mike figured that at this time of day he could make it back to Tribeca, specifically 443 Greenwich Street, in a half hour. That's if he kept a fairly brisk but legal pace, despite the urgency of the task at hand. Yeah, he had to stop the double but he sure as hell didn't want to run into any more cops tonight. No punctures, no road accidents and not even the end of the world itself could hold him back. He had to reach his apartment before that *thing* walked into his home and took possession of his life. Failure was not an option. If the double won, then it would be an instantaneous ride back to the dark woods for Mike. Straight back to Hell.

He gripped the wheel, damn near strangling it. He kept a close lookout for any silver Genius Cars on the road. Genius Cars were rare enough that Mike didn't think it would be hard to spot one, especially at three o'clock in the morning.

He glanced at the knife again. It's petite and ornamental stature sugarcoated the grisly task that awaited Mike in

Greenwich Street. He still didn't know for sure if he had it in him to kill. Sure, Anita said it wasn't a human being – it was a spell in the shape of a human being. It was Lindy and Roz's creation, a trick, an illusion. Not real, not real. Fleshy pixels. That's all he was doing, correcting an error that if left to run its course would see his life in ruins. This wasn't killing a man, not really. It wasn't murder.

He had to protect his family.

From Yonkers, he took the 9A direct to the city. He was back in a world of color again – color and bright lights. It was dizzying. And when he reached the outskirts of the city itself, it had never looked better. Mike had often cursed New York and its bloated emptiness – Ancient Rome with iPhones sounded right, but not now. Tonight, the Big Apple felt like an old friend he'd taken for granted. The Hudson River to his right and the high-rise buildings on the left – they were perfect. They'd always been perfect. Even the billboards looked like angels from a distance.

He wanted to scream. He wanted to beat the shit out of the steering wheel. The fucking Gordon family had treated him worse than the worst criminals in the world and for what? For breaking up with someone, something that happens all the time, all over the world. For monsters, the Gordons had pretty thin skins.

"Cool it man," Mike said, glancing at his face in the mirror. "Not now. You gotta cool it. Got a job to do."

He wasn't Mike Harvey, the movie guy. Not anymore. Couldn't be that guy, not tonight. He was a stone-cold killer, midnight assassin and destroyer of nightmares. That sounded better, right? The magic of the Gordon sisters, as powerful as it was, could go fuck itself.

Despite the urgency, Mike kept within the speed limit all the way back to the cobblestones of Greenwich Street. The cops wouldn't be shy about pulling over a black man in a fancy car at this time of night. The panic was spilling over as he reached the familiar streets of Tribeca. Where the hell was the double? Was it over already? Was he too late? Mike drove slowly down Greenwich Street, pulling into the side of the road and that's when he spotted another car parked further down with the lights on, engine still humming at a low volume. Might be a cab, Mike thought at first. An Uber?

No, he told himself, killing the engine and lights. That was a Genius and there was someone inside the car, sitting bolt upright in the driver's seat.

He'd made it, just.

Both cars were parked a short distance from the handsome, seven-story red brick building that Mike called home. The home that Lindy and Roz wanted to take away from him.

Mike slid down a little on the driver's seat. Probably no point in trying to hide. The double had surely noticed the other Genius pulling up nearby a moment earlier. Or did the *thing* even care? Did it even have a mind of its own or was it just the Gordon sisters' puppet? The double was so close to fulfilling the task – all he had to do was get out and set foot in the building and it was over. Mike would plummet straight back to Hell. Back to the drums, the blackface dogs and all of it. Eddie's ghost would be resurrected and his name dragged through the mud all over again. Then it would be Mike's turn.

Jesus, those Harvey boys turned out bad, didn't they? And they had all the advantages too. Just goes to show...

No, Mike thought. They wouldn't get away with it this time. No more framing the Harvey boys.

He watched as the taillights on the other Genius were switched off. The driver's door opened slowly and the double stepped out, as casual as if he'd just gone for an early morning coffee run. Looking at him now, Mike saw nothing that would arouse suspicion in the people that knew him best. Anita was right – he *was* Mike.

The double began to walk towards building. His shoes scraped over the cobblestones like two rakes.

Mike's jaw hit the floor. He couldn't believe how brazenly the son of a bitch was walking towards the door. Like he really did live there.

"No," he said. "No you don't."

Mike grabbed the dagger off the seat and felt a surge of adrenaline coursing through his veins. So be it, he thought. Murder it was.

14

———

"Hey," Mike said, rushing towards the imposter. "Hey asshole!"

Although trying to catch the double's attention he also wanted to keep his voice down, not wanting the neighbors to flock to their windows in droves. He didn't want anyone to see this. No one wanted to see this – whatever the fuck *this* was.

"Where do you think you're going?"

The double stopped and turned around. The shit-eating grin that Mike saw on his face was a kick in the teeth, as if his sudden appearance was of no consequence to the double's mission. But it didn't last long and the gleeful expression at first shrank to a smirk, then all that remained was a look of of mild confusion.

"How did you get out?" the double asked. "How did you even get out of there?"

Mike walked towards the other version of himself. Kind of like charging towards a giant mirror in which the reflection didn't move. Light raindrops landed on his head, falling from a dark, menacing sky that lingered over his apartment building.

"I said, where do you think you're going?"

"I'm going home," the double said, jerking a thumb towards the building. "But you knew that already, didn't you?"

"The fuck you are," Mike said. "That's my home. *Mine.*"

They stood at the intersection of Greenwich and Vestry Street. The entrance to the apartment building was only a short walk away.

"Well," the double said, waving at Mike. "It's been great catching up with you, but I'd best be getting home."

He turned his back on Mike and resumed his trek across the cobblestone road.

Mike felt like he'd been slapped on the face "Hey!"

Panic spilled over, and he charged forward without a plan. The cold indifference of the double had Mike so worked up that he forgot about the knife he was carrying in his right hand. He lunged at the double as if to rugby tackle him and felt a solid, brick-like fist slam into the center of his face. Everything went black and for a moment, New York City was spinning like a disco ball in a seventies nightclub. When the lights came back on, Mike was sitting on his backside on the ground, a stream of blood gushing down his nose.

Wait.

He gasped.

His right hand was empty. The dagger, he'd lost Anita's dagger. Mike searched frantically but he couldn't see it anywhere on the cobblestone road that was peppered with fresh raindrops. The damn thing was small and it was dark, but why couldn't he see it? How far could the dagger have gone? Mike glanced at the double, trying to push back the tsunami of terror rising up inside him. Had the other Mike seen the weapon? Had he picked it up already?

"Oh shit."

Mike felt like he was sinking. Drowning thirty feet above sea level. The fight, if he could even call it that, was over already and whad'ya know? He'd blown it after one lousy shot. Anita had offered him a chance to get out of the dark woods and Mike had royally screwed it up.

The double stood over Mike, a giant looking down upon an ant. His gloating eyes were shaped like Mike's but there was something missing. It was as if someone else was in there, sitting in a tightly-packed control room with a specialist crew of sick and twisted minds, operating the double and making it do all this heinous shit.

"Mike Harvey," the double said. "Mike Harvey likes to hurt women."

Mike was still trying to flow the stem of blood leaking from his nose. "What the hell are you talking about? You're the one that kicked the shit out of Anita. I watched you do it."

The double laughed and then stopped abruptly, as if he too didn't want to arouse the neighbor's attention. "We're not talking about that," he said. "You're kinda stupid, aren't you Mike? We're talking about breaking our sister's heart. Do you really think you'll find someone better than Anita Gordon?"

Mike squinted. "We?"

The double's eyes were swirling like two kaleidoscopic lenses.

"Lindy?" Mike said. "Roz? Are you in there?"

The double grabbed Mike at the back of the shirt collar.

He tucked his fingers inside and pulled hard, bunching the shirt up around Mike's neck. The double shifted his grip, tightening the collar choke like a jiu-jitsu master going in for the kill. Mike's throat seized up as he was yanked to his feet like he weighed no more than a toddler. The double released the choke and threw a hard hook to the body. Mike saw the punch coming but he couldn't get out of the way in time. It landed hard. Felt like the double's fist rammed straight through him. He gasped for air and staggered backwards. Another vicious blow to the ribs left Mike feeling like a tree that had been chopped in half. The double's strength was not the strength of an ordinary man, that much was for sure. A straight right to the temple sent Mike crashing backwards and he didn't even register the impact as he hit the road. Looking up, New York was full of stars, both in the sky and on the street. Most of them however, were in orbit around Mike's head.

He urged his battered spirit to keep moving. To keep fighting back even if it was a lost cause. All he could do was scramble back to his knees, feeling like someone crawling over the deck of a ship in stormy waters.

The double crouched down beside Mike. There was a disappointed, almost bored look on his face as if he'd hoped Mike would put up a better fight.

Mike could vaguely hear a wet, spattering noise. The rain was getting heavier.

"This has been a lot of fun Mike," the double said in a blunt, mocking tone. "And although we'd love to stay here and beat the shit out of you all night, that's not why we're here. Is it? We're not here to let you off the hook with a good ass-kicking. We're here to destroy you and your family."

The double straightened back up. His expression bore a hole through Mike's head.

"You should have taken our advice. If you'd just slipped a rope around your neck and joined your kinsfolk in the trees, none of this would have happened. It's really most unnecessary. Now, we'd better go claim our space, before someone sees us. See you back in the dark woods Mikey. See you real soon."

Mike rubbed a hand over his numb jaw.

"Crazy bitches."

But the double was already on his way, walking towards the apartment building. He wasn't even breathing hard while Mike lay flat out, a bloody and battered wreck in the middle of the road. His tongue slid over a warm and wet gap in his mouth. The bastard had knocked out a tooth.

He could hear the drums again. The dark woods were calling.

"No."

Drawing on his reserves, Mike pushed himself back onto his feet, swaying like a drunkard as he struggled to stay upright.

"Lindy!" he called out, no longer caring who heard him. "Roz. You asked me a question. Wanna know how I got out of the dark woods? Well, I'll tell you right now. It was Anita – Anita released me and sent me after your skinny white asses. She sent me to stop you ruining my life. What does that tell you? Huh? Tells me your sister loves me a hell of a lot more than she loves you."

He laughed hard, even though his ribs burned. He wanted them to know that, even though he was beat up, he wasn't beat.

The double stared at Mike with those hazy eyes. "You're lying."

"You know damn well I'm not," Mike said, the taste of coppery blood in his mouth. "Deep down, you know the truth. How else could I have gotten out of there? Not on my own steam, that's for sure. And why else would she do it, huh? Lindy? Roz? Why else if she didn't love me more than she loves you? Ha-ha!"

There was a blur of movement. Sounded like a horse galloping towards Mike, the beat of the hooves in perfect time with the drums in his mind. Mike yelped as he felt something like a train crashing into him, throwing him backwards onto the road. He landed in a crucifix pose, arms and legs stretched to the sides.

"Uggghh."

His body couldn't take much more punishment. He was starting to feel like one of Anita's coffee cups on the kitchen floor, broken into a thousand pieces. Didn't even have the voice left to scream.

Mike's arms and legs wavered in the air. He looked like a bug trapped on its back, unable to turn over and get moving again. Pain signals traveled through the axon to his brain, overcrowding it like a horde of trains flooding the station at once.

He heard the angry, scraping footsteps of the double getting closer. Sounded like a giant rat scurrying in his direction. Mike tried to flip himself over but he couldn't. His mind was still in the fight, but his body was waving the white flag, telling the brain it was done. Mike continued to flap his arms, trying to move and just as he was about to give up, he felt something cold at the tips of his fingers. Something metal.

"Holy shit."

Mike reached for the dagger, wrapping his fingers around the narrow handle. That was the boost he needed to get back to his feet and stay there, even though the entire city of New York felt like a giant merry-go-round.

The double marched towards Mike, stiff and upright. It was as if Mike's revelation about Anita had destroyed his – *its* – ability to mimic Mike's walk.

The rain was gushing down in the city. New York was trapped under a blanket of thick black rainclouds.

"I know you're both in there," Mike said, stretching to his full height so that the double was no longer looking down on him. "Lindy and Roz, I've got something for you."

He showed them the dagger.

"How do you like 'em apples?"

The double's face shriveled up in terror. The reaction was powerful and jarring, like a dog smelling a lemon for the first time. It was beautiful and more than enough for Mike to know that, whatever was in the little dagger, Lindy and Roz could smell it. Maybe it smelled to the Gordons like the dark woods had smelled to Mike.

Mike felt a renewed surge of strength in body and spirit. His heart pounded as the blood pulsed through his veins. Yes, he could do it. He could wipe out the double and break the spell.

Get out of the dark woods.

The double's head tilted to the side. His eyes bulged.

"She gave you that? She gave you THAT?"

The voice was Lindy Gordon's. And it was the voice of outrage.

Mike walked the double down, the dagger held aloft, ready to strike. The double backpedaled in a jerky creeping motion, a low-pitched moan of dread spilling out like a leak. The face contorted wildly. Mike saw Lindy Gordon in the face, then Roz, both sisters' faces superimposed over the double's features in a trippy collage of eyes, noses and mouths. Both witches were screaming, desperately trying to push their way out of the double as if they were trapped inside a stringy bubble, one that wouldn't pop no matter how hard they pushed or clawed at the surface.

Mike devoured every second, watching as they tried to flee the prison that they'd created. He realized then he was looking at young, clumsy witches. These were not seasoned professionals and at that moment it didn't matter whose blood flowed in their veins. They'd fucked up. They hadn't prepared a swift exit should the double's body come under threat.

Too confident. Now they'd pay the price.

Mike plunged the dagger into the double's heart. He shoved it in deep and winced at an explosion of piercing white light that formed a silver arch around the thrashing double who was drowning on dry land. Lindy and Roz Gordon screamed in high-pitched unison, both trapped in the arch of light.

Their screams however, were lost in the torrential rain.

Mike fell backwards onto the road, shielding his eyes from the fireworks. He heard a noise that sounded like two balloons popping and then the light and arch were gone. There were only the two Gordon sisters, lying flat on their backs in the middle of the wet road. Lindy and Roz wriggled around like fish stolen from the water. Gasping for air. Their faces were unrecognizable, so bent and twisted out of shape that they appeared to be aging decades in seconds. Mike watched from afar. It was fascinating. A horrifying sight – so horrifying that he began to question what he'd done.

Had he merely broken a spell? Or had he actually...?

"No," he said, shaking his head. "No."

Lindy and Roz Gordon, two-thirds of pop sensation Flaming Candy, gradually shriveled up into old, disfigured crones. Their gnarled fingers reached for Mike. Their eyes, full of hate to the end, never left him. Lindy (or was it Roz?) tried to say something but before the words came out, both sisters were swallowed up by the road as if pulled down into the depths by something big below.

And the rain fell harder.

15

Mike got back to his feet. He picked up the knife and stood there, waiting for the Gordon sisters to explode through the surface of the road. Reaching for him with their gnarled claws and screaming 'GOTCHA!'.

Didn't happen. They were gone.

The downpour over New York was outrageous. Raindrops, violent and murderous, crashed to Earth like boulders.

Mike paid little attention to the weather. He couldn't quite process what had just happened outside the apartment building on Greenwich Street. Were the Gordon sisters dead? Like, really dead? He'd come into this fight believing that the dagger was a spell breaker and nothing more but thinking about what he'd seen moments earlier, the two sisters and their gruesome demise, that looked pretty final.

"Holy shit."

He had to get off the street. Mike hurried back to the Genius, grabbed his jacket from the trunk and zipped it all the way up to his neck, covering every inch of his bloody shirt. The rain had washed most of the blood off his shirt and pants but he wasn't about to take any chances going into the apartment block. A bloody Mike, staggering through the door at this time of day wasn't a good look.

There were two security guards that alternated night shifts at 443 Greenwich Street and whichever one was on duty, Mike had to convince them it was business as usual. *Nothing out of the ordinary here my man*. With any luck, Mike thought, Sam would be working tonight. The other one, Bob, was in his thirties and he was more eagle-eyed than the sixty-something Sam who was more mellow than his younger, more ambitious colleague. Sam was pretty much an ex-hippy who got on well with everyone. Bob was the sort of security guard who thought he was a cop. And not the good kind.

Mike grabbed some Kleenex from the glove box and wiped off any lingering traces of blood on his clothes and skin. Christ, he was sore. As he slipped the dagger into his jacket pocket, he looked over to where Lindy and Roz had shriveled up into nothingness. He could still hear their tortured screams.

He crossed the street, hurrying towards the building before he drowned. He noticed that the double's Genius Car wasn't in the parking spot anymore. There was only a gap in between the other vehicles.

He ran to the front door, peering into the well-lit reception area. There was no one at the desk and the door, as always at this hour, was locked.

Mike rang the buzzer and it wasn't long before Sam's head poked out from behind the wall at the intersection of corridor and reception. He stared at the front door with a bemused expression and when he finally made out who it was, hurried over towards the entrance. Thank God, Mike thought. Detective Bob was having a night off, probably watching CSI repeats at home in his underwear, twirling a plastic pistol around his trigger finger. Sam's face, gray bearded and kindly, lit up and Mike could hear the security guard apologizing as he typed the code into the alarm and then released the deadbolt. He pulled the door open and Mike stepped inside, his clothes dripping onto the floor. He was barely listening to Sam as the old man explained how he'd been on a bathroom break and that he'd only been gone from the desk for a couple of minutes. Then he said something about getting Mike a towel. His voice sounded distant, most likely because Mike was still out there on the street, fighting the other version of himself.

"You want that towel?" Sam asked.

Mike blinked. His attention returned to the security guard and he saw the concerned expression on Sam's face. "Huh? What'd you say?"

"You're soaked to the bone Mr. Harvey. I feel partly responsible, not being at the desk and all when you needed me. Can I get you a towel? How about a hot cup of tea or coffee?"

"I'll be fine," Mike said, his jaw throbbing. "Think I'll just go straight up Sam, get out of these wet clothes, pour myself a drink and hit the sack. Been a helluva long day man."

"Sure thing," Sam said, stepping out of the way and watching Mike walk towards the elevator. "You'll catch your death if you don't lose those clothes soon."

"Yeah, I know."

Mike, his damp clothes clinging to his skin, did his best not to limp. He pushed the button and waited for the elevator doors to open.

Sam waved. "Sweet dreams Mr. Harvey."

"Night Sam."

The doorman was still waving as the elevator doors opened and slid shut again. When they finally closed over, Mike collapsed against the mirrored wall, barely able to stay on his feet. It wasn't just the physical trauma. He was trying to mentally process everything and even now, he still couldn't rule out the possibility of a bad dream.

The elevator stopped at the fourth floor and Mike, his gait a little stiffer now that no one was watching, labored down the hallway to apartment 4C.

"Oh God," he said, convinced that his bones were about to snap. Mike made a mental note to guzzle a shitload of calcium supplements for the next month at least in order to aid his physical recovery.

4C. He was home at last.

Mike unlocked the door and staggered inside his four-bedroom apartment. 4C boasted high ceilings with original wooden beams exposed, dating back to the early twentieth century when the building had been a functional ware-house for a book bindery company. That was before its transformation into luxury apartments. 4C effortlessly blended elements of the rustic and urban modern, and Mike had fallen in love with it at first sight although he'd viewed several other apartments on the fifth and sixth floor too during his one and only viewing. It cost a ridiculous amount of money, fifteen million dollars, and that was something he wasn't comfortable telling people (and boy did they ask!) But it was home. He was a Tribeca boy at heart and for the foreseeable future, Mike had no intention of moving anywhere else.

It felt great to be back.

"Lights," Mike said, hobbling into the living room. The ceiling lights responded and a pale glow trickled down as he labored over the oak floor and made his way towards the drinks table – his favorite part of the room. At least today it was. Hands shaking, Mike managed to pour a large Scotch and devoured it without even tasting it. With great effort, he poured another, spilling precious liquid all over the floor.

"Oh God," he said, draining the second glass and wiping his mouth with the back of his hand. "What happened tonight?"

Nothing made sense. Nothing would ever make sense again.

How could it?

He glanced out the window, his exhausted eyes looking down on Greenwich Street. There was no sign of a disturbance out there. Looked normal. The rain was still crashing down from a black sky and from up on the fourth floor it looked peaceful. Like the water was washing everything clean.

Mike was almost out on his feet when he heard a knock on the door. At first, he thought it was the rain thudding off the roof and didn't respond. The second knock was louder. Closer. Mike's standing slumber was gone and his body stiffened.

"It's Sam," he whispered, putting his glass down on the table. Jesus, his hands were shaking again. Heart pounding.

"It's Sam." The sweet old ex-hippy, as forgetful as he was, had neglected to give Mike some mail, a message or whatever else had been dropped off for him earlier in the day. It happened. Or maybe he was just bringing Mike that towel after all. Or a hot coffee. Still feeling guilty about not being at the door when Mike was trying to get inside. That was Sam, he was considerate like that. Sensitive.

Besides, who else would be knocking on his door at this

time of night? At this time of *morning*? Mike didn't want to think too much about the possible answers.

Another knock.

Mike crept towards the door, hoping that whoever it was, they'd go away.

Third knock. Loudest one yet.

"Who is it?"

"Hey," Anita said in a quiet voice. She knocked gently this time. "It's only me."

Mike almost fainted with relief at the sound of her voice. He limped over, released the chain and when he pulled the door open, Anita was standing in the hallway, smiling at him. She was in perfect color this time, casually dressed in a pink t-shirt and ripped jeans. Looked like she'd come over for a night of TV and beers. Her clothes, Mike noticed, were bone dry.

"Holy shit," she said, her smile fizzling out when she saw Mike. "You look like you've just been fished out the Atlantic Ocean. On top of that, you've probably aged sixty years in one night. Your nose is bleeding babe, are you alright?"

Mike's voice sounded hollow. "I'm fine. I did it just like you said. I killed the double before he could get in here and yet...I killed *them* Anita. I think I might have killed Lindy and Roz, for real."

Anita's expression was blank.

"I thought the dagger was just a spell breaker," Mike said, spitting out words in between short and shallow breaths. "I didn't realize that it would..."

Anita walked past Mike, entering the apartment. She closed the door behind her and pressed a finger to her lips. "Fix yourself another drink babe."

"No," Mike said. "You're not listening." He put his hands on her slight shoulders and gave them a shake. "Do you understand what I'm saying? You gotta hear me right now. I think there was more in that dagger than you first thought. Lindy and Roz, they're dead. I stood out there in the street, in the rain, and watched them die."

Anita wriggled free of Mike's grip. She went over and sat down on the couch, parking her backside on the edge of a faux suede cushion. "I conjured the dagger," she said in a slow, careful voice, "I know exactly what it was capable of."

She coughed into the back of her hand. "Damn, I hope I'm not getting a cold. It's so wet out there tonight."

Mike stared at her. Did she not understand? Was she in shock or something? She was sitting there on the couch, carefree like it was any other night. TV and beers. Every-thing about her was somehow...*different*. Even the way she was sitting was different. Her posture, it was more alert. More grown up. This wasn't quite the woman he'd known and been intimate with for the past four months.

"Anita," Mike said. "Why are you smiling?"

"Am I?"

"Yeah."

Anita cracked her knuckles and Mike winced at the popping noise her joints made. He'd never heard her crack her knuckles before.

"You did good tonight babe," she said. "Really good. A-plus, top of the class, take a bow and all that good stuff."

"Anita," Mike said. He heard a hint of desperation creeping into his voice. A crack at the edges. "What are you talking about?"

Anita got up and walked over to the drinks table. She poured herself a large Scotch, took a sip and her face wrin-kled in disgust. "Acch, that's gross. How do people drink this stuff and pretend like it's okay? Like it's cool. Might as well be drinking piss."

"Talk to me Anita."

She sighed and put the glass down on the table. Then she leaned up against the window, watching the rain, speaking in a quiet voice.

"It's like I told you back there in the woods Mike. I can't interfere with my sisters' magic, at least not directly. The rules man, the fucking rules. They're my blood and it's not permitted. Not only can't I interfere with their work, but I can't kill them either. You know, if I wanted to. Can you believe that? It's dark magic and you can't kill whoever you want to kill. That's bullshit, if you ask me."

She turned her back to the window. Now she was facing Mike and her eyes were burning blue fire.

"Kill," Mike whispered. "Kill your sisters?"

"Yeah," she said, taking a step forward "I would've done it myself if I could. Swear to Daddy."

Mike felt like the room was spinning. "Anita, you're freaking me out."

"Thing is," Anita said, her voice flat and bored-sounding. "I'm sick and tired of the whole Flaming Candy thing. *Flaming Candy this and Flaming fucking Candy that.* I'm sick of it. I'll be thirty in six years or something like that and what then? I'm supposed to keep acting like a teenage pop princess all my life? Do you know what it's like being me Mike? My fate was decided before I was even born, scribbled on the back of some five-dollar notebook that my mom picked up in Kmart. We had no choice. Mom sculpted us – the singing, eating healthy like it was a religion, staying away from other people in case they distracted us with parties and drinking and drugs. No friends, no adventures, no life. I couldn't breathe man, I couldn't fucking breathe. But you know what I really hate? I hate having two other people in the world who look and sound exactly like me.

They're with me everywhere, all the fucking time. Like two shadows I can't shake off. When they breathe it feels like they're stealing my oxygen. Let me ask you something – how is anyone ever supposed to feel truly special when there's two other people like them in every way imaginable? Huh? You know how it makes me feel having Lindy and Roz around? Makes me feel disposable."

She exhaled and her eyes cooled to their normal shade of blue.

Mike felt lightheaded. He'd backed away towards the door without even realizing it, but Anita was quick. She was a blur of motion, standing in front of Mike and blocking the exit before he knew it.

"What are you doing?" she said. "I haven't finished talking yet."

She was smiling. Her squeaky-clean smile, the one the cameras loved so much.

"What's going on Anita?"

"What's going on," she said, "is a great launch for a solo career."

Anita's eyes gleamed with excitement.

"Think about it," she said in a curt, metallic voice. "Think about the headlines a few months from now, okay? Anita Gordon bounces back from family tragedy. Is this the greatest comeback in the history of pop music? You know how that old story goes, right? Boyfriend murders girlfriend's sisters and then kills himself. Shock horror, scandal, all that headline-grabbing good stuff. The person that comes back from that sort of fucked up tragedy is going to be welcomed with open arms. Guaranteed number one single, number one album. Life story, documentary – the works. I'm telling you Mike, the outpouring of love I'm going to get will be insane."

"What the hell are you talking about?" Mike said. "You're crazy."

"Maybe," Anita said. "But it doesn't matter because the public will be all over me like a rash. When I come out of the grieving period, let's say a few months, I'll be able to do anything I want. I could hit a drumstick off a crack pipe and it'll still be number one. The sky's the limit babe. A talk show, podcast, movies and best of all, no more sharing the limelight with the two lookalikes. We're no longer one person with three heads and I owe it all to you Mike. Thank you so much for all your help."

She pointed at the window.

"Unfortunately," Anita said, "the final act isn't pretty. I'm thinking that you were so guilt-ridden after the double murder of Lindy and Roz Gordon, that you opened the window and took a big fat header onto the sidewalk. Brains splattered everywhere. Messy, but it'll be quick too. You won't feel a thing."

Mike stumbled onto the couch. He barely noticed that he was off his feet.

"It was you," he said. "You did this. You did everything."

Anita nodded. "Ta-da!"

Mike could barely get the words out. "You were never pissed off about me flirting with that waitress tonight," he said. "That was just the first part of your masterplan, wasn't it? Stage one, and then the rest of it. Proudfoot pulling me over, the dark woods, everything that happened out there – it was you. How could you? How *could* you?"

"It was nothing personal Mike," Anita said, hands up in the air. "I just needed a tool that's all. Someone to do what I couldn't do myself because of the rules. That's where you came in. I spent four months getting to know you, learning what buttons to push and it didn't take too long to figure you out. Man, you're an open book. You're wary of cops. You're mildly claustrophobic. You've got all that racial tension simmering that I suppose all black people have deep down – I remember us talking about old movies and you telling me how all that blackface stuff freaked you out as a kid. I didn't even know what blackface was but Google's your friend, right? I thought I did a pretty good job designing the dogs. And then there was the Eddie material, oh boy Mike. It was like panning for gold every time we talked after sex. And I'm a good listener – don't you think?"

Mike seized the arm of the couch, gripping tight. He was certain he could hear the drums again.

"You were Proudfoot?"

Anita stood at the door, basking in the afterglow of a job well done. "I was all of it babe. I was the dark woods, the Klan, the hounds – everything you saw except my sisters. They were real, but they didn't know they were in my world. They thought it was Daddy's world. And that reconstruction they showed you, your double beating up my double, that was their own work. Not bad, not bad at all. I knew they'd bring something nasty like that because Lindy and Roz never did like you. And once their plan was in motion, I knew I could bounce you off that plan and that you'd do anything to stop what they'd started. Especially if your family's reputation was at stake. You're a good boy Mike, you love your family and you want to protect them from another Eddie scandal. It's admirable."

Mike shook his head. "Does your *Daddy* know what you've done?"

"Daddy's busy," Anita blurted out. She took her back off the door, hands glued to her hips. "You think he's got time to worry about all this? Anyway, I think he'll appreciate the artistry involved. I went to a lot of effort to pull this thing off."

"You orchestrated the death of two of his daughters," Mike said. "You don't think that'll piss him off?"

Anita shrugged. "Shit happens. Daddy knows that better than anyone. Hell, most of the time Daddy *is* the shit that happens."

The front door was still off the chain. Mike saw it and thought about making a run for it, but even if he could get past Anita and outside onto the street, he knew he wouldn't get far. She was a monster for God's sake. Her power was unimaginable, even if she did have the maturity of a spoiled teenage brat.

Anita tilted her head, throwing out the little girl lost look that drove her fans wild. She pointed to the window again. "Let's get this over with, huh? I'll let you do it yourself if you want. For old time's sake."

"Jump?" Mike asked. "You want me to jump? Thanks, but no thanks."

"That's absolutely fine," Anita said, walking towards him. Her sneakers were silent on the wooden floor. "I'll take care of everything. Hey, at least the black guy didn't die first this time. Hmmm? You get to go last. See Mike, I'm not a racist."

Mike waited until she was closer. Then he whipped out the dagger and pointed it at her. There was no trace of the double's blood left on the blade – it had been washed clean in the rain.

"Remember this?" he said, stabbing the air, testing Anita's reaction. "Huh? Did you forget about this and what's in it? Well, guess what? Maybe I don't wanna be the final move in your twisted chess game you crazy bitch."

Anita's face was a mask of horror. Mike knew he had her.

He realized in that moment that Lindy and Roz weren't the only young, overenthusiastic witches who'd made a miscalculation. While Lindy and Roz had gotten themselves trapped in the double's body, Anita had forgotten about the dagger. The dagger that killed witches.

"Give me that," she said, shielding her eyes with her hand. "You're messing with power that you can't possibly comprehend."

Mike was grinning like a maniac. "Yeah, I guess so. And judging by the look on your face, *baby*, what I'm holding right here is a piece of motherfucking witch kryptonite. That sound about right?"

"Mike," Anita said, her body sagging towards the floor. Her voice sounded like it was shrinking inside her. "Y-you've seen what I can d-do. That was just a w-warm up. I can do a whole lot w-worse and I will if you don't get that d-dagger out my face."

He spat at her feet. "Do you know what you put me through tonight?"

Anita raised her arms to the sides like she was about to sprout wings and take off. Her eyes turned jet black – the same color as the sky above the dark woods.

"GIVE ME THE DAGGER!" she roared in a voice that wasn't human.

Mike stood his ground. "Fuck you! I saw what this little knife did to your sisters. Wasn't pretty, just like falling out of a window isn't pretty."

He charged forward, ready to die if he had to. Mike plunged the dagger into Anita's heart, ramming it deep into the flesh. Anita's doll-like body shuddered upon impact. There was a sudden, scalding pain in Mike's hand that forced him to drop the hilt. He backed away, a plume of steam coming off his hand.

"Aghhh!"

Anita's body shook feverishly, arms still stretched out in a rigid crucifix pose. Then she stopped dead. Not blinking. Not even breathing by the looks of it. She was like a statue of herself standing in the middle of Mike's living room.

Laughter.

There was a sizzling noise, the sound of a frying pan on the stove. Mike watched in horror as the blade, trapped in Anita's body, began to disintegrate before his eyes. Tiny pieces of metal, bone and steel broke off, crumbling into dust. In the end, all that was left of the weapon was a spiral of black smoke floating up towards the ceiling.

Anita tilted her head sharply to the side and Mike heard the crack of joints snapping. Her laughter grew louder, more ferocious.

"You don't pay attention," she said in a mocking tone. Her eyes were blue again, thank God. "Do you?"

Mike tried to speak, but couldn't. His mouth opened and closed like he was trying to impersonate a goldfish.

"The dagger can only be used once," Anita said. "I told you that. Think of it like a honey bee stinger. Or if you prefer, like a solid insurance policy on my part."

"Damn," Mike whispered.

She smiled. "Yeah, I'm not quite as dumb as my sisters were. Having this sort of power doesn't mean you get to stop using your brain. For example..."

Anita screamed. It was loud enough to wake up everyone in Manhattan.

"DON'T KILL ME! DON'T FUCKING KILL ME MIKE!"

"What the hell are you doing?" Mike said, hands clamped over his ears. "Are you insane?"

The screaming stopped. Anita shook her head, smiling her pop star grin again. "That wasn't me," she said. "That screaming you just heard was Lindy and Roz pleading for their lives before you killed them. Now your neighbors will testify to hearing screams coming from your apartment in the early hours of the morning. This eliminates the need for a thorough investigation. Most cops are lazy anyway – they'll be happy with the story I present to them. Less paperwork, more coffee and doughnuts."

"That's so fucked up," Mike said.

"What can I say? My mom was a planner and I'm a planner too."

She was pointing at the window. "You still have to play your part Mike. Let's try again, shall we?"

"Wait!"

Mike felt an invisible force slam against his body, throwing him halfway across the living room. He landed on his back, winded and feeling like he'd been chopped in half. There were family photographs flying around the living room, caught up in the storm. Mike saw pictures of Eddie in school, gap-toothed grin and dimples. He saw his parents on their wedding day – June 25th, 1977, so happy and young. Mike raised his head off the floor. Anita wasn't even doing anything; she was just staring at him through two black holes again. The force continued to push Mike backwards as he flipped over onto his chest, fingers clawing at the smooth surface in search of something to grab onto. But the harder Mike resisted, the more Anita pushed and her power was beyond him. It sounded like a hurricane was trapped inside the apartment and Mike was swirling around inside the eye.

He heard a scraping noise over the storm. Looking back, he saw the window sliding open, as if guided by an invisible hand.

"Jesus Christ!" he yelled, clawing frantically at the floor. "No! No!"

His fingernails screeched off the wooden surface. Sounded like he was raking them down the surface of a neverending blackboard. Mike screamed and cried out for help. He battled the storm but it was too strong for him and whatever meager resistance he had left in the tank, it was dwindling. He'd survived a lot of shit tonight but this last fight he couldn't win. Anita would have her scandal. She'd have her glorious redemption, her new career as a solo star and Mike's parents would have their shame, forced to live with the stain on his reputation and the broken hearts that would surely follow. A lie, just like the narrative around Eddie's death. But a lie his mom and dad would have to live with.

The rain was louder. He felt the morning air, cold and bitter, snapping at his back.

Closer, closer.

He was almost outside.

And then it stopped. The storm cut out and Mike heard all of the objects that had been lifted into the air crash back to earth with a bang. A few things hit him in the back, but Mike didn't care about that. He was alright. He was no longer fighting to stay inside the apartment. Looking up from the floor, he saw that Anita's concentration had been interrupted by an unexpected sound, and there it was again. A knock on the door. A calm, gentle knock that pushed Anita's hurricane aside like it was nothing.

Mike's face fell flat on the floor. Underneath the couch, he saw a coat of dust and a lemon candy drop that he'd lost three days ago.

He heard the front door creak as it opened.

"No," he said, his lungs burning. "Don't come in." Mike knew that whoever was about to set foot in his apartment would never walk back out. Anita wouldn't allow it. She wasn't about to leave any witnesses that could testify to her presence in Mike's apartment at this hour. There wasn't a rich asshole from Tribeca alive, man, woman or child, that was going to get in the way of her redemption story.

Mike's heart fluttered when he saw Sam's head poking through the gap in the doorway.

"Is everything alright Mr. Harvey?" the security guard asked, casting his eyes over an apartment that looked like it had been turned upside down.

"Sam," Mike said, trying and failing to climb back to his feet. "Sam, get out of here. Just go, just walk away. Everything's cool man, I promise."

But Sam didn't leave. With that genial smile on his face, he opened the door further and strolled into Mike's apartment like he had nothing better to do. He took in the sights, including the fully open window on the other side of the room that was leaking rain into the apartment. His nostrils twitched as he inhaled the residue of black smoke that lingered in the air.

Anita faced the security guard, which meant she had her back pointing at Mike. Oh shit Sam, Mike thought. He'd at least tried, hadn't he? Tried to save the poor old bastard from being massacred. He couldn't remember if Sam had told him about his family – a wife, kids, grandkids, all who'd be left to grieve the kindhearted old man after Anita nuked him as she was surely about to do.

Sam closed the door behind him. At the same time, Mike heard one of his neighbors, Matt Johnson, screaming down the corridor towards 4C.

"HARVEY! Keep that fucking noise down! Some of us have to work in the morning, you hear me? Fucking Hollywood moron, I'll shove that Oscar so far up your ass you'll be shitting gold for months. KEEP IT DOWN!"

"Sam," Mike said, ignoring his neighbor's abuse. "Don't come in here. I told you. Open the door and just walk man. Just…"

His nostrils flinched. His apartment was suddenly filled with a foul, violent odor that had nothing to do with the black smoke. It was like nothing Mike had ever smelled before and he gagged on the scent.

Sam slid the chain through the track, securing the door. Then he turned to face the others, his face a picture of serenity.

"Sam?" Mike said. "What's going on?"

Sam didn't talk. He was looking at Anita and as he did, her shoulders began to tremble. It was subtle at first, then it picked up speed. Her arms, legs and the rest of her body were shaking too. The strangest thing of all was her blonde hair, standing upright as if an onslaught of static electricity was concentrated around her head.

Mike was back on his feet. Wobbly, but stable. The room didn't just smell horrible – it was cold, quite possibly the coldest space Mike had encountered in his life. All the bright colors of his apartment, the paintings, the furniture had faded to gray. Like a giant shadow had been cast over the apartment.

Sam glanced over Anita's vibrating shoulder. "My apologies Mr. Harvey," he said. "It seems my girls have caused you no end of trouble tonight."

Mike's jaw dropped. "Sam…"

"Not Sam. Or rather, Sam is not me – I'm merely borrowing this body and voice for a short time in order to sort out this mess."

Anita continued to shake like jelly in between Mike and Sam. Her feet were rooted to the floor.

Sam walked into the living room, passing the vase of

butterfly orchids that Mike's mom had recently given her son as a gift. The orchids flopped dead and turned gray.

"My girls are blessed with unimaginable power," Sam said, strolling back towards Anita. He looked at her through the eyes of a disappointed father. "And yet Mr. Harvey, they have no idea how to use it. They waste it on petty causes – fame, followers and nothing of substance, at least as far as I'm concerned. And tonight, the eldest of my triplets used her power to trick you into killing her sisters for her. Her blood, my blood."

"*Daddy*," Anita gasped. Her voice was the breathless wheeze of a hundred-year-old woman on her deathbed, fighting to get her last words out. "*Please stop...*"

Sam blinked in her direction.

Anita's feet left the floor. Now she was levitating three feet in the air.

Mike heard a sharp clicking noise that sounded like a light switch being flicked on. There was a deep-pitched whooshing noise that felt like tremors inside the apartment and the flames, when they appeared, started at Anita's feet. The flames raced up her body and that's when she began to scream. Her body twitched but she couldn't move otherwise. The flames hurried up her jeans, a hot trail of destruction moving at speed, ravaging her neck and head. Mike watched in terror as his ex-girlfriend's face shriveled up like a piece of paper in a campfire, turning charcoal black and disintegrating into a thousand fragments that floated around the room like snowflakes.

It all happened in about ten seconds.

He dropped to his knees, burying his face in his hands. He didn't need to see any more. Didn't want to see it.

When Mike finally found the courage to look up, there was no smoke. Anita was gone and there was no sign that she'd ever been there in the apartment. There was only Sam, standing at the door with the chain now unlatched, his wrinkled fingers flirting with the handle. The look on his face was grim and unapologetic.

"May I ask you a question Mr. Harvey?"

Mike's lower lip trembled. What would happen if he said no? He was pretty sure this *presence* inside the apartment wasn't used to anyone saying no.

"Sure."

"Do you have any children?"

Mike shook his head. "No. I don't."

Sam nodded. "You want my advice? Keep it that way. Kids, they're much more trouble than they're worth. And they're into such weird things nowadays – I can't keep up."

He sighed, partially turned towards the door and then stopped. He spun around to face Mike again.

"And now Mr. Harvey…"

Sam's fingers slid off the metal handle. "I'm sure you understand that nobody who sees me lives to talk about it. Yes? The more invisible I am, the better."

Mike recalled the famous Baudelaire quote, popularized by *The Usual Suspects*: 'The greatest trick the Devil ever pulled was convincing the world he didn't exist.'

"Yeah," he said. "I guess I was hoping you'd forget about that one."

They stared at one another across the room. The silence that accompanied this exchange seemed to last forever.

"And yet," Sam said, "it's against the rules to kill our own."

"What?" Mike asked.

Sam pointed to the open window. "Anita would never have tried to throw you out the window if she'd understood. And you Mr. Harvey, you would never have attempted to harm my two daughters if you'd known the truth and might I add, it's only your genuine ignorance of the matter that has spared you suitable punishment."

"I don't get it," Mike said. His head was spinning. "My genuine ignorance of what?"

"We do not kill our own. That's what will save you tonight. And for the record, Anita's not dead either – I didn't kill her because she's blood and it's against the rules. She's simply coming with me for a while. As for you…"

"Me?" Mike said, his heart thumping against his rib cage. "I'm not one of you."

Sam leaned into the dim light from the ceiling. The light shrank as if afraid of the presence. "Think carefully Mr. Harvey. I think you'll find otherwise. I know there's a drop of my blood in your body – do you remember how it got there?"

Mike clamped a hand over his neck. It felt like he was choking on something that he'd consumed a long time ago.

"No," he said, his insides clenching up. "You can't be serious. That was just a bit of stupid, meaningless fun. It was Anita's idea – I didn't even know who she was at the time. *What* she was. I thought she was…no, that's not fair. It's not fair. You can't hold that against me. You can't!"

"Relax Mr. Harvey," Sam said. "You've been inconvenienced enough as it is tonight. Let me assure you that I have no plans to call on you again. But you might want me to. That drop of blood we spoke about is not like any other drop of blood you possess. It will never leave you. I will never leave you. You can always call on your father if you need him. If there's something you want – another Oscar perhaps or a certain Officer Cecil Proudfoot to meet a slow, grisly end, all you have to do is ask. There's nothing that cannot be arranged. At a fair price, of course."

Sam's final words were a whisper.

"Goodnight Mr. Harvey."

He left the apartment and Mike stared at the door, numb and beyond exhaustion. Somehow, he was able to limp back over to the drinks table where he opened the sixteen-year-old Lagavulin. He drank from the bottle.

As he drank his way to oblivion, Mike heard angry voices and footsteps thundering down the hallway. Moments later, the mob had gathered outside 4C and somebody was pounding on the door with heavy fists, cursing Mike and yelling all kinds of obscenities. It was Matt Johnson, yelling at the top of his cracked, high-pitched voice. Johnson thumped the door some more, telling Mike in no uncertain terms what he'd do if the smug Hollywood son of a bitch didn't keep the noise down and let him sleep.

Said he'd give him Hell.

THE END

OTHER BOOKS BY MARK GILLESPIE

If you love taut, fast-paced, claustrophobic horror, you'll love The Hatching

'A pulse-pounding post-apocalyptic horror series.'

The Dystopiaville Omnibus: 'Think Twilight Zone or Black Mirror, but with books...'

After the End Trilogy (Complete Box Set)
'These are the best of the genre.' - Kindle Reviewer.

'Civic terror, apocalypse, gangs, horror, complete decline of civilization...read it and weep!' - Mallory A. Haws

The Future of London (Books 1-5)

Butch Nolan wants revenge. And not even the end of the world will get in his way.

The Complete Butch Nolan Trilogy

THE EXTERMINATORS TRILOGY

Black Storm

(The Exterminators #1)

Black Fever

(The Exterminators #2)

Black Earth

(The Exterminators #3)

"Part-horror, part post-apocalypse...all brilliant."

DYSTOPIAVILLE

Is this fiction? Or is it the future?

Shut Up and Die!

WaxWorld

Killing Floor

All Dystopiaville books are stand-alone novels/novellas that can be read in any order.

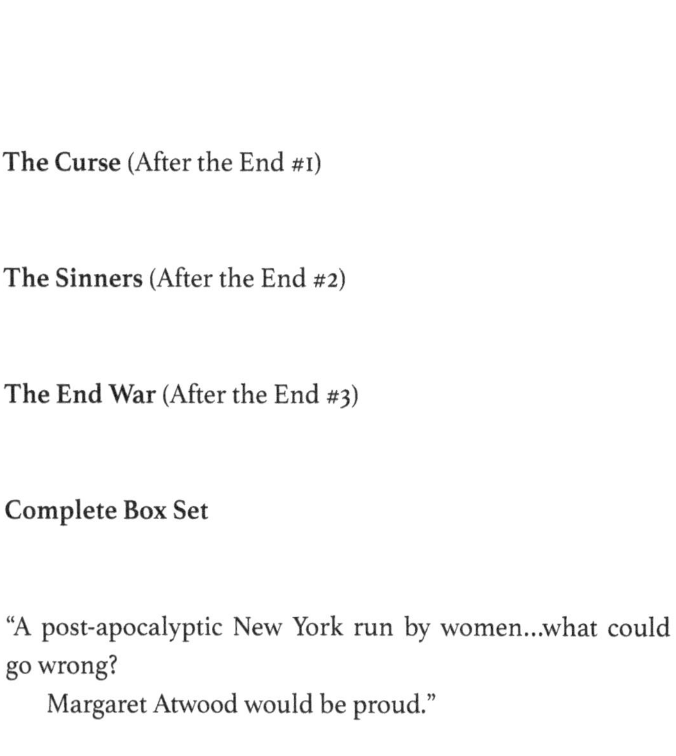

AFTER THE END TRILOGY

The Curse (After the End #1)

The Sinners (After the End #2)

The End War (After the End #3)

Complete Box Set

"A post-apocalyptic New York run by women...what could go wrong?

Margaret Atwood would be proud."

THE FUTURE OF LONDON

L-2011 (Future of London #1)

Mr Apocalypse (Future of London #2)

Ghosts of London (Future of London #3)

Sleeping Giants (Future of London #4)

Kojiro vs. The Vampire People (Future of London #5)

The Future of London Box Set (Books 1-3)

The Future of London Box Set (Books 1-5)

"Modern dystopian at its very best." - Kirsten McKenzie, author of
Painted.

THE BUTCH NOLAN SERIES

Nolan's Ark (Butch Nolan #1)

ManHunter (Butch Nolan #2)

Deathflix (Butch Nolan #3)

Mad Max meets John Wick meets Clint Eastwood's spaghetti westerns in this rollercoaster ride of a post-apocalyptic action thriller...

GRIMLOG (TALES OF TERROR)

Apex Predators

Air Nosferatu

Rock Devil

"What's not to like about zombies and sharks, or zombie sharks?" - CJ (5 stars)

"Brilliantly fast-paced horror that was unputdownable." - Chantelle Atkins (5 stars)

JOIN THE READER LIST

If you enjoy what you read here and want to be notified whenever there's a new book out, join the reader list. Just click the link below. It'll only take a minute.

www.markgillespieauthor.com

(The sign up box is on the Home Page)

You can also follow Mark on Bookbub.

WEBSITE/SOCIAL MEDIA

Mark Gillespie's author website
    www.markgillespieauthor.com

Mark Gillespie on Facebook
    www.facebook.com/markgillespieswritingstuff

Mark Gillespie on Twitter
    www.twitter.com/MarkG_Author